Erasable Strokes

Erasable Strokes

Tales Brought by the Crows

by Jez Levi-Tate

First edition.

For **Misaki, Shiori and Leon**,

When things seem dark and inexplicable,
You never know what is around the next corner.

And for **Douggie G**,

My partner in crime in the Japanese suburbs,
From Oregon to Ōfuna, time and distance are illusory.

Table of Contents

"A cage went in search of a bird" (Franz Kafka)

Preface: Words Brought by the Crows

It was as though the stories were brought to me by the crows.

The pages that turned up on my doorstep were, of course, put there by the delivery man. As I opened the door to see what he had left there, however, I saw that a large murder of crows had assembled on the little front lawn.

I thought, "Hitchcock!"

They all seemed to be angling their beady side-eyes at me. In that moment, there seemed no doubt in my mind that they were focussed on me; they weren't going about other, normal crow business. Well, it would come to seem prescient.

I had that feeling of wondering if I was dreaming …and knowing that I wasn't.

On the doorstep, between me and them, lay a large package. I retrieved it, took it into the kitchen, wondering what I had ordered and forgotten about. I took out a manuscript, loosely bound with twine and, I thought, smelling of smoke?

It was typed in Japanese. I knew very well the little mazes that formed each word, transporting me back to another time when I had been a young man with big dreams and the world at my fingertips, I'd thought. I sensed, instantly too, who had sent me this package.

Two drop-outs we were: I met Naoto 'Keshava' Karasuma on the Masters degree in Creative Writing we had both enrolled on. He had a light frame, floppy hair, died light brown at that time, and his nervy laugh and good nature were contagious. His English was almost flawless, but for an obvious accent; he'd spent time in Canada and England. He was adept at both Chinese-style ink painting and fiction writing. He'd travelled to India as a sixteen-year-old and stayed there for five years (where he accumulated the moniker *Keshava* from one of his guides – my *spiritual name*, he told me), seeking some sort of spiritual enlightenment through yoga and retreats with various gurus. I don't think he had achieved it, had grown disillusioned with some of the masters' questionable ethics, and had returned to Japan, enrolling on the course where I met him. (In a partnership between British and Japanese universities, I spent the first year on exchange.)

In the university refectory, we used to talk over endless cups of coffee that left my nerves jangling and my brain firing on a thousand cylinders. That was attributable not only to the caffeine but also his head full of hundreds of artistic ideas. I sometimes thought that his biggest obstacle was that he had too many interests; he couldn't narrow them down to one, and focus on it. That would have meant missing another opportunity.

And sure, enough he didn't last beyond the second semester, his attentions and priorities suddenly elsewhere. We had studied the Beat writers together (see his story in this collection, *Inerasable Strokes*, for evidence of his interest in that genre) and then contemporary Japanese literature in our second semester – at which time, I decided to switch to translation and interpreting. (I wasn't as creative as I'd hoped and preferred a more pragmatic and guaranteed income.) He also bailed on the course, and later on I heard that he had gone to stay in a Buddhist temple in Ofuna, where the Kannon-sama statue, in brilliant white, looked down on the surrounding suburbs and countryside with compassion – an incredible, larger than life tribute to world peace, an unparallelled conceit of iconography.

Keshava wrote to me once from the temple, for those were the days of letter-writing, and I wrote back to him, but there the trail ended and I never heard from him again. This was more than twenty years ago and I wish I had the letter to publish along with these short stories of his, but it was a victim of a flood in my basement.

More correctly, I should say that I didn't hear from him until this collection of stories landed on my doorstep. There was no accompanying letter this time with his news, nothing but a very short handwritten note – perhaps evidence of some Zen Buddhist minimalism he had acquired! It said, in English:

When the reader is ready, the story will appear! Please set fire to these words.
Or else translate and publish.

And so here they are. You can see the choice that I made.

These tales are sometimes dark and strange, heirs to Kafka, Dostoyevsky or Edgar Allen Poe, and they frequently wander into the surreal, bedfellows of Murakami or Auster, but however tormented and bizarre, to my mind there always remains some golden thread of hope running through their core.

Knowing Keshava as I did, and his quest for some kind of blissful enlightenment, his constant search for the story that told his truth, his paintings of ethereal, inky ghosts in mists beside temples, I like to think of the stories in this collection as *spiritual horror* stories, if there can be such a thing, or perhaps *zen gothic,* with their supernatural twist. This is my own description, and readers can make up their own minds about what they represent and the truth that they seek to tell.

You will find stories about writers searching for stories, or losing them, characters in need of words that elude them, troubled souls who seek escape from prisons, real or imagined, and you will encounter a recurring theme of characters who are not haunted by ghosts so much as that they *want to* see ghosts, they want to find a plot, or perhaps just something more profound and meaningful than the reality they already know. Doubtless, you will meet many crows, a recurring theme of Keshava's. (His family name, Karasuma, written 烏丸 in Japanese, does after all mean crow circle, so perhaps it should be no surprise to find a book littered with crows here and there.) And, of course, as per any good set of gothic tales, you might well encounter some actual ghostly or supernatural figures, some more apparent than others.

I have titled the collection *Erasable Strokes* as they arrived at my door with no overall title. One of the short stories is called *Inerasable Strokes,* depicting the practise of sumi-e ink painting in which nothing is changed once painted, a spontaneous, zen-like way of creating that features more than once in this collection. (This was also the premise of much of the Beat writers' work, for example Jack Kerouac's *spontaneous prose,* also mentioned in this collection.) At the same time, some of the stories concern words that cannot be found or slip away from sight, and *Erasable Strokes* seems to encapsulate that, whilst also nodding to the ghostly themes and lack of permanence elsewhere. The subtitle *Tales Brought by the Crows* describes how they seemed to appear with me, out of the blue, almost as though those crows outside were responsible. Their arrival was much like the strange occurrences in these stories – and it seems fitting to give a mention to those enigmatic birds that swoop through so many of these tales, almost heralding the descent into insanity that these characters often experience.

If my choice of title isn't perfect – for I am not a writer or the author of these works – I console myself that at least it is a better outcome than burning everything.

In order to remain as close to the original as possible, I have retained the division of the short, journal-like narratives, *Finding the Plot,* each part accompanied with a time of day (*Midday, One o'clock*, etc), even though these form one complete story. This is how they arrived at my door, separated into times of day and interspersed amongst the more regular short stories. This was one of Keshava's early writings and I recall him discussing this concept with me over coffee and cigarettes (oh, those times long gone when we smoked as though it were quite normal and chatted uninterrupted by the ping of a mobile phone or the bleep of a smart-watch!). Through the fog of years, I seem to remember how he told me of his plan to visit different locations at different hours of the day and night and pen (in the days when writing was largely executed with pens) a paradoxical story in which a narrator, battling alienation and doubting reality, drifts high and low searching for a story but cannot find one (although of course, he *is* writing it). Slave to his quest, he wanders compulsively like a hungry ghost. Keshava well understood the sense of alienation of living overseas due to his travels abroad. Clearly, this story evolved, after we had talked about it, and grew to include a rather different, more ethereal narrative.

Our discussions were all in conversation and sadly I don't have any written evidence of this, so I may have misremembered and adjusted my recollections after the event. At any rate, it seemed fitting that he interweaved this narrative with the more regular short stories. In my opinion, this narration, together with the stories that follow each one, make for a balanced whole.

I have not altered any of the content of the stories themselves. I have translated them and, like any good translator, aimed to stay as close as possible to the text whilst also retaining the spirit of the originals.

One final point of note is that I did attempt to find Keshava's whereabouts before embarking on the work of translating these stories – and again before publishing them. I contacted the temple in Ofuna where he had once stayed and was informed that he had long since departed. They didn't know where he had gone and, knowing his itinerant and spontaneous nature, who knows?

I like to imagine that he has given up worldly aims and retired to a mountain temple in the remotest part of Japan, or China, or India, where he meditates and bestows positive vibrations on humanity, and perhaps paints inky representations of the stories he wrote or the truths he has uncovered. I can imagine with equal ease that he might be filling cars with petrol, slicing fresh fish for sushi at a restaurant counter, or fishing in a little boat in Hokkaido. I hope he has found what he is looking for – and I hope that, in the stories that follow, you too find what you are looking for.

It has now been several years since I tried and failed to track Keshava down, and proceeded to translate and publish these works, as I believe that these stories deserve to be seen.

Deepest thanks to Aiko Inoue at *Machine in the Ghost* for illustrating the cover, the Table of Contents, Franz Kafka quotation, *City Man 1, City Man 2* story and the story divider icons.

Any errors in translation are mine.

Trelawney Beito, Translator, September 2024

Finding the Plot

Midday: The Search

Seya Ward, Yokohama, 1997

I'm a writer. But I don't have a story.

I lay down my fountain pen on top of the notebook, noticing that it never seems to run dry any more. The news is on TV, telling a horrible tale of someone's senseless murder, a teacher in his twenties. I can't shake the feeling that I've heard this before. It's as though I've dreamt it. Deja-vu, I suppose. Well, the news is always repetitive, a cycle of horror.

The poor guy even looks like me, in the mugshot they flash up, smiling away without a care in his young world.

Over a lunchtime coffee in the Missing Bean *café in central Yokohoma, a stone's throw from the university, Mickey instructed me to start writing. He was a Canadian colleague with the resourcefulness and optimism of Dostoyevsky's* Razumikhin, *whereas I was, I suppose, mooching around in the manner of a* Raskolnikov. *Okay, I wasn't about to bludgeon an old woman moneylender on the head with the back of an axe but I had been feeling pretty gloomy, lost in a haze that sometimes made me forget when I had last slept. Or eaten.*

Mickey, as well as playing guitar in a band that did little gigs at a local bar, wrote down his thoughts every day. He had stacks of filled notebooks that his wife was curious about, but he showed to no-one; he didn't even re-read them himself.

I think he was a little worried about me. I'd told him how I felt empty after the exit of my fiancée for a presumably more romantic, or maybe just less bird-minded, French guy. My mind was like a crowd of birds, on the ground, pecking at grains of rice. That was what I told him. I didn't bother going into the debts I'd acquired from my recently deceased father, and the discouraging prospect of repaying those for the foreseeable future. I hadn't even been close to him. I think Mickey got the general picture, though, just from looking at me.

With an undaunted grin, he told me that we never know what is around the corner, what fresh adventures and new events. And he told me to start writing every day.

"Write what though?" I had asked.

"Anything. Everything. Start with whatever you see, just describe it all. Write down all your thoughts about life, death, the universe. Try it! You'll find it a wonderful experience, I'm sure."

I had obeyed his instruction and soon words were queueing up for my pen's attention. It seemed as though I was depicting a record of my experience, trying to find the bright light that animates it all. And there was something about it that did seem to bring me back to a more colourful life. I'd take my notebooks with me as I explored my surroundings. They were a camera pointing inwards, taking snapshots of my brain.

And despite, or because of, the warnings of my ex-fiancée on several occasions that writers hanged themselves and that I had better stop quickly, I continued.

"They always meet with sticky ends," she said.

"Which writers are you thinking about?" I asked.

"All of them. They're dead inside, so it never ends well," she said, which seemed extremely harsh and not at all accurate.

I tried to make light of it. "I don't think so, Sweetheart. I'm sure lots of writers are happy."

She shrugged. "It's a waste of time, anyway."

And that was probably what she had meant to say in the first place.

My days had lacked purpose ever since Sandrine had upped and left, in any case. It wasn't for nothing that Mickey had told me to start writing. And my pen gathered more and more steam.

And then I stopped.

I'm not quite sure why. Something must have happened in the background or in my psyche. Perhaps there was a change in the weather or it was the revolving seasons. Some force had stopped me in my tracks. I'd lost the spark. Sometimes I would be writing in a café and, looking up, it would be empty, time having flown and I would have an empty page, nothing written. I found myself questioning whether I had written certain pages at all.

The world had felt a little muted of late, as though I was standing just outside of it, looking in, without truly participating. I wanted to start again but I needed to work out what had gone wrong. I decided that, this time, I needed to find a story worthy of telling.

I would write something more significant than just my own mundane musings. Not just a record of my own quivering existence, but a more poetic insight, however minute, into how it feels to live, before our candle is extinguished and the mysterious, dark void of the unknown eats us up.

I was no storyteller, though, and I didn't know how to write such a story of dramatic worth; I was a teacher, eking out a humble existence at the university, striving to make lessons a little less boring for my oversized classes of students. A good lesson plan was the extent of my creativity.

Zero storylines had whistled through my brain during the course of my hectic working days, but having got into the habit of writing, I was resolved to continue with my plan. Write about what you know, they said, the imaginary experts and gurus concealing themselves behind black typeface. I decided to use the simple but true story of myself.

I might not exactly be a Dostoyevsky anti-hero – and I was glad of that – but I'd search for a story. Raskolnikov wasn't the only character capable of being a man on a mission.

And now to find inspiration worthy of a story is my quest. I resolve here and now to go in search. It must be out there, amongst the buildings of the city, or in the walls of the temple up on the hill in my neighbourhood, or perhaps lurking in the little forest below the temple. I'll seek it out, round the clock, until I find it. Hour by hour, day and night, I will go to the locations where a story might reveal itself to me. This is my resolution and my responsibility, I decide.

I consider the fluttering, small birds outside my cold, sliding door. And I remember that in life, it's a good idea to find something you really like doing, and always pursue that thing. I'm grateful that now at least I have a purpose – a pick-me-up to replace my departed lover: to find a story, perhaps one that will even tell its tale so that it grips and sings to its reader, and not disappoint, like so many potentially great stories, and lives, with its ending.

> *Crispy, blue autumn skies*
> *Hanging above yellow trees*
> *Can fill you with tears;*
> *It comes to my stifled thoughts:*
> *Life's worth living after all.*

Losing the Plot

I'm a writer.

I write words (when I'm not cooking noodles or sprinting up staircases in the direction of shrieks).

Some of those words are good and some of those words are bad. ...Or shall we say that they are 'less well developed'?

One thing is for certain: the words I grind out, once written, remain where they are on the page. That, after all, is the normal order of things.

And that was always the case until the day that it wasn't the case.

What made it worse was that the story I was working on was about the meaning of life, which I had just worked out! In a Kafkaesque nightmare, a painter finds himself trapped inside a coffin for no reason at all. It turns out that the coffin is not buried in the ground but resides in an eerie graveyard on top of a hill in the suburbs of Yokohama, Japan. As he puzzles over how this has happened to him, he is led to search for the real essence of painting – and the real essence of life – both of which he learns from a gravedigger-cum-retired ink painting master. (Spoiler: He finds that the two essences are inseparable.)

At the moment of epiphany, just as I had laid the final words like the final heap of soil on a freshly filled grave, I saw the words I had just carved with black ink from the depths of my subconscious twist and squirm, as though there was a leak in the ceiling and the rain was pouring in and disfiguring them. They didn't remain atop their neat lines in my notebook, but slid silently to the top of the page, and from there off the edge, as though into the vortex of a black hole. Aghast, I could only stare.

When it was too late, I came to my senses and grabbed both edges of the notebook, peering over the top of its pages, searching out my precious words, which were...

…Nowhere to be seen. I might as well have lain on the edge of a cliff, trying to spot the smallest fish in the roaring ocean below.

On the retina of my eye there flashed for a fraction of a second the after-image of those words disappearing into a crack in the table.

Like a madman, I scowled into the congealed dust and rotted crumbs in that forgotten groove in the wood.

And I saw nothing but blackness.

As though someone had run into my house and slapped me hard around the face, then run back out again without a word, I shook my head and laughed in disbelief. It wasn't funny.

I threw down my pen and thumped the table hard with both fists.

It was one of those moments that make you question your sanity. Because it's so inexplicable, you resign yourself to it and carry on as normal.

Maybe it was some kind of optical illusion.

I decided to make a cup of coffee and write the words again, as best as I could. And that was a logical idea. The only problem was that when I sat back down at the table, and grasped my pen, and looked at the blank page, I couldn't re-create those missing words. However I tried, they weren't right, they weren't the same, something had changed.

(And what if I did conjure them up again, I thought; would they slip off the page again?)

At that exact moment, there was a rapping on the front door. At first, I had to strain to hear whether it was indeed a rapping on the front door, or an echo from my rage, or something my wife was doing upstairs.

The light, urgent knocking came again.

There was noise and activity all around now, the stillness of my inner world dispelled (along with the words that had come and then gone). Mandy was coming down the stairs with the deafening silence that her zombie-like movements inflicted.

"Who is it?" she called in a monotone.

I went and peered through the spyhole.

There was no-one there.

"Kids," I muttered.

Just to check, I opened it anyway. Perhaps someone had come to return my missing words, or I had won the lottery that I never bought a ticket for, or there was a mystery that needed my urgent help to solve it.

No-one there, I thought again, but then saw a figure bending to lay something against the wall beside the front door.

She stood up. "Oh, hi," she said.

She was pretty, with large-framed, rectangular glasses, futuristic-looking clothes and hair that was both long and short in a punk kind of way.

"Hi, can I help you?"

At her feet, I saw a square package, propped against the wall next to my front door.

She had on red and white high heels with a harlequin pattern.

"I think you've got the wrong house," I added.

"I brought you this." She indicated the wrapped object at her feet.

I couldn't find any words – again. (Some writer I was!)

"It's for you," she said, helping me out. "You'll need it."

"What is it? I don't want it." That was a lie. I did want it. I was intrigued. This was just the kind of mysterious little event I wanted.

With a smile, she turned to go. "It's a painting," she said matter-of-factly.

"I haven't ordered anything."

"Present!"

"But I don't even know you," I tried, although I didn't run after her as she disappeared down the path in front of the house and closed the iron gate behind her.

She looked over her shoulder once more and said, "You do now."

I watched her all the way to the end of the road. She had a nice shape and there was something about her manner that was very appealing.

In spite of the weirdness of the situation (and everything that was happening this evening), I bent down and picked up the package and took it inside.

I placed it on the table (scene of absent words) and carefully untied the string and opened the corners of brown paper.

The 'painting', if it deserved to be called that at all, was a black square. Thick strokes of black ink that had erased every speck of white canvas. There was no subject – unless the subject was a black hole …or the darkest night …or the concept of Nothingness.

Then came the incident with Mandy's birds. It was like an after-cursor. Or maybe I had cursed her. That was how it seemed.

I heard her screaming upstairs. It came out of nowhere.

I'd been cooking some spaghetti (like a character in a Murakami novel), checking that it wasn't too al dente (unlike a character in a Murakami novel). I liked it soft and almost mushy. Boil the shit out of it, that was my philosophy.

I dropped a wormy strand into the cauldron as her shriek pierced the peaceful torpor of the suburbs.

I burst out of the kitchen, took the stairs three at a time.

Many things had gone between my wife and I, and many things that ought to have gone between us had not, but a cry like that from *anyone* demanded either that you sprinted to their rescue or that you crawled into a cupboard under the stairway to hide.

I flung open her bedroom door.

It was like a scene from a bizarre dream, from a tormented surrealist painting.

And although it was terrible, and she would never be consoled, it was not as terrible a thing as I had feared. That isn't to say it was fine and dandy, just that from the noise of her screams I had imagined her being murdered or raped or brutalised.

The cages of her numerous birds were where they always were. But each and every one had an open door.

Those grills that cornered her pets exactly where they had to be stood nonchalantly open.

"You!" she screamed at me and I could see the way this was going to go.

I didn't bother to reason with her. I didn't bother to console her. I had given up on those kinds of things a long time ago.

But this wasn't one of her ordinary tantrums; that much I could see.

"Calm down. What's happened?"

She screamed at me. I could see flecks of spit firing out from her wine-stained lips like laser beams. "Don't tell me to calm down. They've gone! They've fucking gone! They've all f-f-fucking gone!"

I surveyed the room. The windows yawned open wide. The cages were empty. One or two errant feathers drifted in the breeze coming from outside.

I wanted to ask what had happened, if someone had been in the room, if she had been sleepwalking again …But there was no point. She had already tried and convicted me, even though I had been far from the scene of the crime, enveloped in pasta preparation, not in the liberation of her aviary – however much I disliked her captured victims, imprisoned with her just like I was.

I had never thought of freeing her birds. But now that I considered it, perhaps I should have done.

…If only they could have freed me.

"So this was your ploy?" She carried on. It was funny how the most manipulative people saw machinations where there were none.

"I was downstairs, Mandy."

She had tears flooding down her rosy cheeks now. I felt a rare compassion for her. For an instant, I saw the broken core at the heart of her soul and I really wished I could help her, that things were not as they were.

I walked to the windows and looked out. The sky was blue with just a few Simpsons white clouds animating its vast expanse. Mandy's birds had well and truly disappeared.

I assumed that she had released them, somehow not knowing what she had done.

I did feel responsible. First the words, and now the birds. It was an echo of my weird fate, a shadow, a by-product of what I'd just experienced.

Later, giving up on missing words, giving up on missing birds, I stumbled out into the fresh, too-fresh air, pulling my coat collar up around my neck like a Noir detective.

If I couldn't find words, I'd find the ultimate coffee. And then, when I'd discovered the ultimate coffee, I fantasised, I'd open a coffee shop and call it *Ultimate Coffee (Mind-Blowing Brews)*.

That was one of my obsessions. I had two. I wrote in search of the ultimate truth, the meaning of life – which I had just unearthed and written down, only for it to slip off the page.

And I explored – in the search for the ideal caffeine brew. I wanted to pin it down, like a butterfly, nail it to memory, refuse to let it fly free; I wanted to cage that taste. I wanted bliss. I wanted love and ecstasy and transfiguration. ...In a coffee cup. And in words.

My life was predictable – but I had found that you could never dip your tongue in the same coffee cup twice.

Now I found myself standing outside the *Missing Bean*, the rain having picked up its sense of urgency. I smoothed my hair, which felt like a drowned bird on my head. Inside, I spied a pretty brunette with a blue apron, her hair wavy and bouncy (as she might be in the sack, I fantasised, loving and joining with me in sacred partnership, agreeing afterwards to become soul mates); she wiped a table free of crumbs, morsels from a muffin or piece of toast that had remained to be swept away, evidence gone, mystery cleared. She coughed, straightened, saw me outside the door and smiled.

In I went, a bell clanging like a signifier for a rainy-day funeral.

I managed to find a seat amongst the other addicts, sneaking into an armchair next to the window. I used my butt to angle it to face the window, let the thick tar wash down the sides of my throat, like rain sliding down the sides of an open grave, saturating the corpse in a box below, satiating the thirst of the demons who lurked there.

A pigeon with a single remaining leg skipped by on the pavement outside, grey bird on grey surface, looking unhappy about his body shape and uneven distribution of weight. I thought of the disappearing birds, Mandy's weird pets. I thought of disappearing words from a page, my surrogate pets. I looked into the whirlpool of black goo and contemplated other things that disappeared: money; love; youth; the spark of life; the shape of cliffs by the sea, washing in, washing out, day in, day out; memory.

But memories didn't disappear, did they? They were relegated to the nether regions of the mind. Still, they existed, waiting to be retrieved, maybe, by the scent of cinnamon in a round room, or the echo of an unusual word spoken in a peculiar tone, or by the stubbing of your toe on a dark brown wooden table leg. …Dark brown wood the colour of a coffin in a downpour.

Grey clouds had welled up in the eyes of the sky, seeming to reflect the grey road and pavement, the grey birds hobbling uneasily around, the grey armchair that my arms rested on, the grey feeling in my gut. I watched as the clouds opened a crack, releasing a sudden deluge of water that made the pirate pigeon hobble out of sight.

The rain looked blue, not grey. I could make out large drops and smaller drops. I watched, mesmerised by the blueness – some drops were navy, others were icy. They gushed downwards, sucked to the ground by gravity and demons. They were a whole mass – a *downpour*, at one and the same time, they were individual meteors of water on their own personal trajectory towards earth, each one distinct and unique.

I began to see the raindrops morph into a different shape, some of them. At first, I thought that I was hallucinating, a function of staring at the constant stream. Some of the droplets grew larger and more globular. I could make out words amongst the torrent: greyish-black words, some back-to-front, some seen from an awkward angle, but others the right way up, as clear to read as daylight, as long as my eyes followed their trajectory: distinctly I watched *screaming*, *grin*, *ecstasy* fly past. I thought I could make out *breathing*, *hillside*, *drinking*.

pound-pound-pounding

no sound

rushing and tearing

panic

neon

I knew these words; they were as familiar as old school friends – the people you knew the best, even if not the most closely.

And then, as though there could be any doubt left, I saw, facing the town hall across the street, the one word that gave everything away:

coffin

I threw my coffee mug to one side. An old woman sitting near me shrieked like a newly-escaped bird. I was out of the door in seconds. The pretty barista's voice called,

"Hey!"

An old man hobbling like a one-legged pigeon along the pavement past the café drew up abruptly to watch me rushing past like an errant raindrop flying to earth. He rested on his walking stick and said,

"Hell's teeth!"

I ran into the road, where my words were settling with the floods of rainwater, queuing up to slip down the metal grille at the road's edge.

"No!" I ordered.

Words were draining away into the bowels of the earth.

On my knees, I watched as for a second time, helplessly, I witnessed my words – *my* words – leaving reality in front of my very eyes.

My hands plunged and grappled at the water, splashing around uselessly.

I saw a *pitch* and a *barking* disappear through the metal slats, washed down like a couple of medicinal pills. *Darkness* slipped from sight, too.

Then it was just rain, bleeding greyly from the sky and bouncing on the street around me, seeping down my collar and dripping coldly onto my back.

The rain eased a little. I got to my feet. A car swept around me, its driver grinning maniacally at me.

The pigeon had slumped outside the café window, its eye staring out into the street, perhaps pleading for help.

Finding the Plot

One o' clock: Forest by Day

Seya Ward, Yokohama

The rain is beating down, but I'm unperturbed with my newfound sense of purpose.

All I need is something intriguing to happen to make it all worthwhile, to give me something to write about.

Not only is it throwing down torrents from above, but a gusty autumness has picked up too, flapping my coat tails this way and that. It feels good to be out in it, surrounded by the wild elements. Few people pass me, no doubt preferring the warm confines of their living rooms.

That's nice. But for me there is a story to be found.

A blustery day will tend to blow away one feeling as quickly as it beckons another, but my resolve doesn't slip as easily as that. I can feel the sense of purpose coursing through me once again.

As though challenged by my determination, the rampant storm now flaps unconfidently, revealing a glimpse of its mortality. It rattles the large steel shutters of a flimsy-looking wooden house, and growls out its name, over-compensating.

I don't know exactly where I am.

In my neighbourhood the houses all look similar – and it wasn't long ago that Sandrine and I moved to this neighbourhood. The longer roads stretch for miles and never waver. The back-streets criss-cross, at right angles to each other, but are too small and identical to mark a route, and as you pass them by you might become engrossed in the colour of a roof here, the shape of a closely pruned tree there, a strange silhouette upon a window, a spacious, sparse garden.

The air is cold and clear. The sun has returned.

Despite heading for a lonely coffee shop, I have taken a wrong turn, and quite by accident I stumble across a small forest. I stride slightly uphill into the sopping, tired trees, raindrops clinging to their branches in the sunlight.

The trees are thin and tall – far away in the sky, unbending, close to their life-giving source. Despite the tints of red, orange, yellow, and the carpet of orange-brown leaves, the overall veneer is of greyness, like a picture that has grown so old that it has turned misty and cold.

Here, it's hard to believe there's been a storm. No wind, no sunlight, no clouds, no rain, no breeze; nothing. Even for sound, it's a vacuum. At the very outskirts of this existence there might be a river of cars, constantly trickling along, but it's barely audible. Occasional leaves flutter to the ground like warm snowflakes, but then stillness again. A bird whistles flatly. A rounded, middle-aged women appears, wheeling a bicycle across the clearing where I'm now sitting. She pays me no attention at all.

The crows have arrived to keep me company, magnificent, wide-winged, squawking black animals, who know to keep their distance from it all. Their sound is a more educated version of a dog's bark, and they appear to know something about it all - our existence - that I don't, we don't, but nervously to keep it to themselves. Coincidentally, in the distance a dog now hollers,

"Hoof, hoof."

He knows as little as me.

When I was walking here, I noticed a man following some way behind, and his appearance unsettled me; he had on a light, black leather jacket, and thin trousers, and his face was so empty and angular I felt as if a skeleton was pursuing me. Then I passed a dry, hard, mean, leafless tree; it looked like an old witch, with fingers clasping, grasping this way and that. As I entered the clearing where I now sit, I was relieved to see he had vanished.

This would be an excellent place to play the guitar or read a book or smoke a cigarette, like a solid and contented man with a hobby, perched upon one of these - seats. They look like miniature, brown Japanese shrines. I'm reminded of the Japanese custom of forest bathing, a kind of meditation that promotes the enjoyment of soothing nature amongst the trees and leaves.

As well as it is for me to balance my notebook on my lap here and describe all of this, it isn't a story. No plot to be found here. I head back the way I came.

A little way along the path, a dog stops and stares me down from a pawful of metres away. It seems transfixed. Its eyes are wide open, alert. I have little choice but to continue walking, steeling myself in case of a sudden outburst of nastiness from this little creature.

A flurried-looking old man, who'd been hidden by the little hill in the pathway, catches up with his pet in good enough time to ward off any unpleasantness, and I thank him. He looks somewhat baffled, as if he or perhaps his pet might have seen a ghost, but he isn't sure and hasn't the time to check, scurrying off on his way.

As I reach the edge of the forest, I glance again at those proud, straight trees so far away up there. Just before I reach the road, I notice a sign at the entrance to the wood, warning of a pervert who has been seen in this forest. Having been innocently oblivious, it gives me a disquieting feeling.

Just now a streak of red paint adorned the final tree I passed, suggesting blood and a story of suspense and death. At least, I thought it was paint.

I'm still plotless; this is not the right place.

Inerasable Strokes

Clack clack clack of the typewriter so old-fashioned and rusted and the words so faint. You can barely see them on the page but it doesn't matter.

"Keep on writing," he said. "Don't hesitate, don't look back – not once." Thwack.

It was easy in the wilderness. Believe me how easy it was. What distractions were there but the wearying heat of the desert sun, a rare scuttling lizard, the rousing smack of the cane?

Only at sunrise did I miss my home, for every night I dreamed of animals as I tossed and sweated in the baking cave-oven where we lay – the soft creatures of London parks and streets, patient daft dogs jogging lopsidedly through Hyde Park in the rain with their owners, too polite to scare the birds.

One time, it did become harder to write. The beatings became more frequent and my difficulty was soon overcome.

Such a beautiful green cane – so discordant with the austerity of the wilderness. Only sign of a material possession he had, the wise man my teacher.

"You must never pause, never stop," he repeated. "How else can you expect to get there?"

"Where am I going?" I asked. Once I had known, but at some point it had slipped my mind.

"You came to me and sought my advice," he said – and sure enough I recalled that distant life, another reality.

True enough I had persuaded my teacher out of his meditative regime of creation. For me, it seemed, he had left behind his sweeping canvases of black, grey and white.

His ghosts haunted me with their burning love letters and simple masks. His temples surrounded me from hillsides in Kyoto. And there were his birds.

I knew more of the truth of all birds when I looked at those pictures than ever from an encyclopaedia or book of birds or even BBC 2 documentary.

I'd never wanted to learn about the creatures. I liked other animals more, but here was something deeper than met the eye. Here was a sum much bigger than the whole of its parts. I asked him to teach me to write.

"How can I teach you to write?" he asked with a bemused smile. "The only thing I ever wrote was my signature at the edge of a picture, and this as much a part of the painting as the ink strokes themselves."

"That is true, I am sure. But I had teachers in London, New York, and even in Paris the home of my namesake Mr Sartre. None of those teachers taught me to write with any effect, though they had all been published in dozens of magazines and reviewed in several newspapers."

He stared at me for a long time. A knowing smile crawled slowly across his face and into his eyes. I waited.

"I see that I will be able to teach you. I will teach you, yes. I see it as in a vision."

I beamed. "When do we start?"

"Today."

Perhaps I frowned.

"There is no time to lose," he said and beat me on the head with the cane – my first encounter. Such a beautiful rod. "You want to learn to write with effect. What effect will be wrought by Delay?"

We left the gallery and took a train to the end of the line, from where we walked until there were no longer houses.

I was thirsty and hungry, so my teacher taught me first of all to eat my fill from berries and to drink water from mountain streams. Good job we were in mountainous country, I thought to myself, and he beat me a second time with that stick.

It was funny, too, that as we walked the water assumed a taste like sugar, whereas before it had been plain old water and nothing more. It was better than whisky this water, yes, nicer than lager in a country pub.

I remember crossing a bridge where suddenly the road heaved with cars.

"The point of no return. You sure you want to do this?"

"Why yes," I said. "That's why I've come this far."

"Better to turn back now – even having come so far – than go on and not truly want to."

"Let's go on," I assured my master.

Rule one was simple enough: he made me tell him every particle of wisdom I had learned from my writing courses – and beat me repeatedly with the bamboo. Beating it all out of me, he said. For the first time I suspected a streak of sadism in him, but that was his business after all.

This process took fifteen minutes.

"That's all?" he asked, eyes popping from his head.

"Yes, I think so."

"Good. The damage is not too serious."

I had my doubts about the second prescription, too. I was sent to lie in the scalding sun for eight hours a day. He said I needed to learn more about pain. And this part was marvellous, I must say. It really worked. Many a time I have been able to draw on the memory of heat ripping my skin at the seams, the utter exhaustion and desperation.

I knew.

I didn't know what I knew but I knew.

So I was ready for part three of the course.

"Keep on writing."

"What?"

Thwack.

"You must keep on writing to achieve perfection, though you can and will never attain perfection, the perfection that you seek."

I nodded doubtfully.

"You must continue without hesitation, but never use the word 'must'. It is so stern and puritanical a word."

"You used it," I protested.

A thwack of the bamboo cane reminded me of my manners. He said I must keep on writing, don't stop, and while I must do that I must not use the word 'must'.

…keep on writing. Heat, sweat. Keep on… buzz buzz turn power on on… though I was blind, I saw the old woman in the mind of my eye – she kept deaf dogs in the hot chocolate swimming pool, floating down down down down in Spirals and I knew my destiny…

It didn't much matter what I wrote, he said, for the style and the form and the wisdom would arrive when they were ready. I was to be the channel.

"Is this how you painted?"

"With inerasable strokes," he nodded, smiling from ear to nose.

Whenever I paused in my labours to let my eyes judge or even savour the words I had rapidly crafted, I would feel the rasping smack of his benign stick across my hands.

"Keep on writing – and never look up at the words you shape, on the page or screen or bus ticket that you set them upon. Never look at your words!"

"But… I must weigh them. I must calculate their worth."

"You must write! Words are worthless. They are weightless, floating free from the mouths of those who speak them. Can you see words in a conversation?"

"Only in cartoons," I admitted.

"Words are invisible." His hand stung my face with a slap for good measure.

"Oh, I had a friend," I remembered, my thoughts wandering back to a classroom in London…

"Don't you be shovelling out stinking great filthy mounds of adjectives, John-Paul," Mrs Higginsock would love to tell me and any other students caught luxuriating in the beauty of the language as ancient, opalescent sunlight sprawled in through the mottled glass.

I could hear where she was coming from. I'd read 'difficult' books with exhibitionisticmeritriciousarabesque and obfuscated adjectives rattling like hailstones on the clear window of my mind.

Jack Kerouac was a member of my class, would you believe it, and he wasn't spared her warning – "You beware of littering the literary path with your strings of sausagey adjectives, Mr Kerouac."

"Well I was working on this thing, you see," he said a little despondently. "It's leaping bumping mad cat jazz spontaneous prose, that's what I call it, Mrs Higginsock."

"Oh Mr Kerouac, please now, do you want to sell your writing or not?" she instructed with benign authority.

"...I had a friend," I explained to my sage in the desert. "Well he was a co-student – he had a rule like yours. He called it spontaneous prose."

"There are no rules."

"Rules are there to be broken."

"Breaks are there to be ruled," I heard him whisper before roaring off into merry peals of laughter that echoed around the steamy cave.

"Yes," I continued, not quite sure of the last remark. "And Jack wrote a novel on a long piece of paper – all one piece – I think he took Benzedrine first. Should I do that?"

"You could do. But I hear it's not a fashionable drug." He was an avid newspaper reader, you see, my wise man. "Better to drink cups of espresso, listen to techno music or rave, something that turns your head in circles."

"Oh, you like techno?"

"No, not I. I prefer Noh dance."

"You don't like to dance?"

"No."

"Oh."

"I drink green tea. I meditate before the painting process travels into my fingers."

"Meditation?" I asked with the same scepticism as if he had belched disgustingly in our small cave. "Is it hard?"

"It's easy. But wrapped in cloaks of difficulty and esotericism by its teachers. A little like your creative writing classes, no?"

"Quite."

We meditated every morning and every night.

Hours, minutes, seconds – they seeped into one like the colours of a fresh Monet left out in the rain.

"This time thing that you notice is no coincidence," he rebuked me, once again and very definitely this time reading my mind.

"It isn't?"

"No." His eyes smiled. "When time crumbles, creation begins."

"That's very interesting."

It was true. In the wilderness there was no time. Only the rise and fall of the sun in the sky. Certainly no watches keeping watch.

But he was quite sure when our time was up. "You are ready now – as ready as you'll ever be," he said.

"I am?"

"I hope my training has worked."

It didn't sound as definite as I had assumed. Were there flaws in his wisdom? Still, I was glad I would meet cats and dogs once more.

"Don't forget what I have told you."

"No, sir."

He gave me his e-mail address and we promised to keep in touch.

"But," I stumbled before we parted, "am I really ready to write magnificently? Like you paint?"

"Oh, rest assured it will take practice."

I nodded with suitable severity.

"And besides… I'm growing a little bored of your payment – sex without love is all very well, but…"

"That's okay. I understand. Perhaps if I had had cash to offer…"

"Goodbye."

A sudden thought struck me as he turned to go. "What shall I write?"

He looked over his shoulder.

"First of all, write of my teachings to you. From there, you will find your own inspiration."

"Okay. I will do that."

"Oh…" It was his turn for afterthought. "Remember, John-Paul… remember this…"

I stood hanging from his words…

"Never look at the words you write. Not until they are old friends with the page. Then you may look at them if you wish."

"I'll try."

I still had secret reservations, to tell the truth. But now I came to think of it, in my endless pages of training I had steadily ceased to pay any attention whatsoever to what I'd written.

"Keep on writing."

"Keep on writing," I agreed.

I boarded the train and slumped into a seat, exhaustion creeping over me now that I had finished my course. I stretched out my legs ahead of me, resting my feet on the seat – but had to move when a woman with her baby sat down.

Waiting for the engine of the train to come to life, I closed my eyes and automatically began to meditate. Tiredness washed over me and I was floating near the borders of sleep. …My mind sorting through images, words, sensations and thoughts from the wilderness.

With a start, I opened my eyes wide.

Immediately I unzipped the cases containing the reams I had written. I took out one notebook after another, leafing furiously through each like a maniac.

Most of my precious books were empty and I knew, now that it was too late I knew what had happened.

I was a fool.

And sure enough he was a wise man.

He had discovered promise in me – real talent.

He'd instructed me in the art of Fanciful Nonsense, led me on a magical trip to nowhere and, like a Svengali, pulled the wool over my eyes with words brimming with sinister hypnotism. …And ultimately swapped the useless pages of nothingness now in my hands for the work I had slaved over in the desert wasteland.

No wonder he had agreed to teach me. It was conceivable that his hidden powers of persuasion had set to work on me the moment I'd sought his help. Or had the idea come to him later on, during our outward journey or once he had set eye on my scrambled scrawlings? Or perhaps at the 'point of no return'?

Keep on writing indeed – to make his fortune, no less!

I laughed out loud at my stupidity, earning a frightened scowl from the woman opposite, although her child googled and laughed at me.

"Don't you see what he has done?" I cried. She got up and moved nearer to other people.

I was a little insane, perhaps, after my solitary stay in the wilderness. Still I continued to talk out loud.

"He has robbed me – and of no mere sum of money. He has stolen my time, my money, he has stolen my body and he has taken my soul too. Demon! Slave-driver!"

I examined the ink-filled books more closely. Here were the first ones I had written. No doubt these were not good enough for him to bother pilfering.

Then I looked at the naked books.

Dejection made my mind wander for a time. Until I sensed a seed of elation, of excitement inside me. What was this? Over what?

The answer was simple. Someone had seen fit to steal my writing. …Yes. I was a talent, a prodigy!

Hooray.

Hate and bitterness and anger quickly returned to fill my head with a nest of wasps. The train was beginning to splutter and whine, stretching itself into the task ahead. It wasn't too late to go back and confront the trickster. But a weary idleness permeated my bones.

And still it wasn't the end. So vehement had I grown that I'd failed to perceive the scratch marks… a ghostly inscription on the white pages.

I took a blank book closer to my face.

I peered at it, not daring to believe my eyes.

My God. I was doubly wrong.

I tried to swallow my words, my thoughts.

The pen had inscribed the pages all right. But so long ago had I run out of ink – and not even noticed this little detail – that… yes, I had the right books in my possession.

No treachery had occurred at all. A measure of hypnotism, but no con.

The books with chains of rich black scrawl inside were the early ones. The others, they had been filled after the ink had all gone. Indeed, there was one book that witnessed the transition, words beginning to fade from sight and finally running out, drying up, dying.

Never look at the words you write, I remembered.

Thwack thwack thwack came the bamboo rod every time my eyes dared wander higher up the page to what had come before. I'd been blinded by sun and exhaustion anyhow.

I looked out of the window of the rushing, thumping train. As we gained speed from the station, mountains and shops on corners of road jumped and whisked past my vision – they travelled so fast that they seemed to disappear before my very eyes.

Finding the Plot

Two o' clock: Church by Day

Seya Ward, Yokohama

To collect my thoughts and prepare to collect the story that awaits, I decide to visit a place I suspect will be a good location for inspiration: the church. There is more suggestion of mystery and drama than in the forest, with its dog-walking and bike-pushing folk. All that bloody history, remorse and pain, the entreaties and bargains made with God.

More to my tastes is the Tao, that energy source, that mysterious power, that paradoxically cannot be named. The flow, the light within darkness, the darkness at the heart of light... But although I lack faith in God, for things have happened that have put a barrier there, I head in its direction.

Maybe old habits die hard.

I push open the heavy, squealy wooden door, and find immediately that this is no cathedral; neither is it one of those badminton hall churches where you can have tea parties and invite God, who will be wearing a woolly jumper, along.

It's hard to see right to the far end and the altar, in this greyish light. The ceilings are distant, black and fathomless. Rows and rows of hard-backed wooden pews almost appear to be bowing in stoic worship, as they face the raised platform in the distance, above which hangs a very large, realistic crucifixion. The figure on the dark brown cross is startlingly bright in his whiteness, and the flecks of red from the torturous wounds seem to glow. His eyes, so calm and saintly, reveal indescribable compassion and despair for the world.

Suddenly there is a shadow moving noiselessly in the gloom. It has long, straight hair and a strong, relaxed build. He is joined by another figure, shorter, more rounded, a female companion, shorter hair than the man. They seem to be facing in my direction. I imagine her to be beautiful and cold, though I can't see her properly. Is he the priest? Will I have to justify my presence there… my beliefs… my existence?

A flapping, clattering sound breaks the stillness. I clutch my heart at the shock of its suddenness. Something in the eaves. I can't see. Bats? Or birds?

The two figures turn abruptly and pass through a silent door in the far corner, and out of sight. I overcome my natural caution and follow them. I pass the confessional box, where countless failings are entrusted. Candles flicker, burning solemnly for passionate prayers.

I reach that door in the corner of the church.

I find the handle.

I'm about to pass through, to seek the story on the other side, when a voice comes from the back of the building, behind me. A shrieking, singing voice, it startles me. One high, sustained note:

"Laaa-aaah".

The single note does not waver. I search the choir's benches on the small second floor for the origin of this melancholy tone from the darkness, and see a woman up there in a long, pretty white dress.

An organ note strikes up and the two merge and become a hymn.

My resolve is drowned out by the noise. Something seems wrong. Something troubles me about being here. It puts me in mind of sombre memories, funerals perhaps. I can't quite put my finger on it and I exit the church and go back outside into the early afternoon brightness and cold sunshine.

Still storyless.

Crime and Misgivings

Raskolnikov fought his way against the wind. It attacked him savagely with the full force it had gathered as it came across the Neva, wanting badly to tear loose his shabby greatcoat and cast the hatchet he had concealed to the ground.

He scowled like the mythical demon bear as he grappled with flapping material, clutching the wooden handle. And despite the coming storm's icy fingers, sweat coated his forehead, the dampness of high fever as his skull pounded, pounded, and guilt already consumed him. If he suffered for his crime now, would his penance be less afterwards?

The starving hamster scuttled frantically around its wheel in his head. He wouldn't do it, certainly not today. He would investigate, that was all. What harm could it do to see the avaricious old sow's apartment one more time?

He gripped the handle more tightly. It was solid and smooth, blade deadly and unforgiving. What if she were alone? She would be defenceless, easy to strike down. He couldn't relent now, no. There was Dunya, not only himself. His anger abated, like a lull in the storm, as he pictured her soft brown hair, pure face so white, dark, innocent eyes. His sister would be saved from a wretched and ill-advised marriage. And with the rest of the money he would finish law school, devote his life to saving the poor - ill, suffering bastards like himself.

Yes, he would do as he had planned, as he had calculated through the twisting, delirious nights consumed with fevered dreams as he had lain shivering. During the day, closeted in his rat-hole at the top of the house, waiting for an opportunity to creep down the stairs past the landlady.

But even now, the wind, like an invisible monster towering ahead of him, hurled itself at him with aggression equal to his. Other people had fled the streets, all too aware of the rolling grey clouds spreading over the city, turning daytime into night. Occasional passers-by stared at him with apprehension, surprised that he dared to challenge the gale, shocked at the deranged determination that lit his eyes.

Raskolnikov crossed the bridge. He felt as if he would be lifted up and plunged into the thick green waters. Holding the railing to his right, he edged his way to the other side, only to be thrown nearly off his feet by an gusty punch that came through the deserted market square and around the corner. But a few feet more and he could see the building, grey block of flats against the grey sky. Not far now. She would be there. He sensed it.

Always there at this time, and with this storm, even more so. Yes, the elements seemed an obstacle but truly they were his ally. If he alone would battle through them to undertake this worthy evil, then all the greater his justification. Few were blessed with the dispensation to commit such a crime without blame. Like a sign from God, the streets in this quarter were deserted but for Raskolnikov.

And then the rain came. Torrents released from on high. Raskolnikov ducked into a doorway, half-drenched already even in the few seconds he had been in the open. Now he pressed his back to the small wooden door, his face but an inch from the buckets of water that hurtled at the cobblestones, spitting up as it hit the street and drenching the bottoms of his trouser legs and his broken shoes.

He cursed.

His second curse seemed to have effect. The rain didn't stop, but its initial wrath was appeased and transformed into a steady flood, still lashing the stones but not with enough rage to prevent him from stepping out of his shelter and proceeding on his way. Water dripped from his soaked hair down his face, and ran down his neck and spine like a malicious insect finding a place to sting. But now it wasn't enough to drench him all the way through, to make him ill – more ill. And now there was no turning back. He tried to ignore the roar of the wind and rain.

Was it trying to tell him that something was wrong? More likely it was a test of his resolve.

But with his agitated eyes fixed to the rain-splattered road ahead of him, and blinded by the grey torrents, deafened by the swirling, screaming wind as it seeped inside his head and echoed there, Raskolnikov failed to see the black horse that careened around the corner, dragging its cart, or its furious driver perched behind the reins, trying to outrun the storm. Raskolnikov heard the beast's hooves, its whine, the wheels drumming on the stones, the cry of the man – "Watch where you're going!" – too late. Looking up in horror, he threw himself desperately out of the way, managed to stagger and fall clear of the racing vehicle, all without losing his grip on the hatchet. Hastily he hid it inside his coat once more, now getting back to his feet and hollering after the horse and cart,

"Watch where you're going!"

"What about you, you bloody maniac?"

Horse's flying steps and the crack of its master's frenzied whip rumbled into the distance, disappearing from sight as if it were a passing dream receding into the dark corners of his mind. Like the dream of the drunken men, roughly beating a donkey outside the inn. Beating and beating it, until they would surely break its helpless back, roaring with malicious laughter at each strike. He remembered that dream now. He remembered it vividly.

He started to walk on, but stopped short and looked down at the drenched side of his trousers and coat, wet with filthy water from the street where he had fallen. But why should that stop him now? He walked on again. It might increase the evidence he would leave in the old hag's apartment. They could somehow trace the dirt to him. He would have to get rid of these clothes, toss them into the Neva.

But even as he drew nearer to his destiny, the rain fell heavily again, the ruthless, insane rain that had first come out of the sky. This was too much. Raskolnikov cursed once more, looking around him again and again for somewhere to take temporary refuge, as he had before. There weren't any doorways. He shouted at the storm. His shirt clung to him, waterlogged coat leaden about his shoulders. There, not far ahead, there was a black, iron gateway on the left. He rushed towards it and through the tiny courtyard on the other side.

Huge arched windows and doorway, a pattern of red and black bricks: a church. He hadn't seen it with his head bent from the rain, his mind on the mad driver of the cart.

Let the door be open...

It gave way to a cold, dry foyer and another pair of grey wooden doors. He sighed at the delay but with relief to be out of the water.

Two sets of doors shut out the howl of the tempest, reduced it to a harmless whisper as though it barely existed. Raskolnikov stood at the fringe of the vast, lofty space, watching drops of water run from his bedraggled clothes onto the cold stone floor, collecting there as he wondered if he could venture any further inside. How long had it been since he had come to a church? Not since his boyhood, when he and Dunya had escorted their mother to the chapel.

How similar the feeling then and now of entering an ornate enclave unlike anything in the world outside its doors. How changed, their happy, simple life before mother had died and the sparse, hungry existence he endured now. Though his family had been poor, he had never noticed hunger, not then. But he had wept even then, walking with his father, as the rough, intoxicated men had scolded the harmless donkey. Had it been only a dream?

The hatchet carefully wrapped inside his soggy coat, Raskolnikov crept further into the centre of the church, huge, high-ceilinged shrine to God. Did he dare to be here with what he was about to do? To set foot here must magnify his crime. And to bring the weapon intended for the money-pinching goat's skull. Raskolnikov forced his eyes to meet the image of the cross, embroidered in thick gold and silver, suspended above the smooth white cloth on the altar. He made for a pew at the rear, fumbling as he sat down, the axe still clutched in his left hand inside its wet cloak, his right hand trembling over the top of it.

It was good to sit. He had been so weary, and hadn't known until now. This smooth wooden seat was the grandest armchair. And so quiet. He could hear the peace ringing in his ears, startling his soul with its immaculate emptiness. Nothingness surrounded him. There was no storm, no horse and cart pounding the street as they ran, no prying eyes of anxious strangers.

The careening thoughts on his troubled mind came to a momentary rest as well. He closed his eyes and ran one hand over the markless surface of the marble pillar behind which he hid, peering around at the front of the church.

There was little Dunya, clutching flowers picked from the roadside. Her hair covered with mother's brown scarf. She gazed intently at the new priest with his long, wild beard and dark eyes which shone with both fire and compassion. It was Easter and still they shivered as they stood side by side, Raskolnikov staring into the fathomless shadows of the church, in awe of the hidden answers that lay there, keeping in his head all the things God expected him to be, and all the promises and hopes of better things to come, one day, in the end.

Raskolnikov shook his head to clear these unwanted visions, the curse of his imagination.

That was in the past, but today he had to collect his wits. He couldn't dry out here in the church. He would only catch his death of cold here. As if to emphasize the good sense of this, a shiver scuttled down his spine. As soon as the rain softened again, he would be on his way. Just a few more moments in the safety of the shadows cast by slender candles on iron racks. He watched their wicks burning softly. Dim rays of light peered through the coloured windows.

The air, pungent with the ghost of incense, took his mind reeling backwards to the standing congregation, their warm breath purified by clouds of smoke swung at them by the priest. Days of innocence. Days of youthful hope.

Hope that had disappeared, yes, like the smoke itself. But there was hope now. No more memories. He must clear his mind. Today Raskolnikov would create hope for his family and for others – students, prostitutes, beggars – who needed money to save them. Kill the old moneylender and put her extorted riches to good use, wads of unneeded roubles lying there in her drawers they were, like some museum artefact that no-one was allowed to set eyes upon.

He examined the simple pictures on the white walls, set at intervals to show Christ in various stages of torment on his journey to Calvary. Then the torturous death. Words from the past resounded in Raskolnikov's ears:

"Christ is risen," the priest boomed.

"Christ is risen indeed," the devoted people echoed.

More words in his mind. Had to think. He let his head fall gently back and eyes swim in the empty space at the top of the church. He sat immobile, transfixed by dark emptiness receding high up above towards the dome-shaped roof, this the dark that must separate the people below from the heavens. His shaking limbs were calmed for a moment. Looking upwards, he was suddenly oblivious to immediate worldly struggle; there were only higher things. His eyes closed peacefully.

He came to attention with a start as the door opened on the other side of the church. A woman shuffled in, her back hunched from age and the pouring rain, grey hair tied back in a thick bob beneath her white shawl.

In terror, he saw Alyona Ivanovna - it was her, his prey. It wasn't possible. How could she be here? He couldn't kill her in here, he realised in panic. But a smile crept across his dry lips.

It would be easy to follow her home and enter her apartment behind her. But why was she here? What did she care for religion or the forgiveness of her soul?

She noticed him as she staggered down the aisle towards the altar, turning her scowling head in slow motion to study him carefully. Raskolnikov drew his damp coat tighter about him, and looked back from under his brow, thinking that she almost seemed to read his thoughts, damn her – but this wasn't Alyona Ivanovna, it was some old woman, another person, come to pay her harmless respects to God.

"Peace be with you," she murmured in a small, sincere voice.

"And also with you," he replied automatically.

On she staggered, right to the front, kneeling and then clambering onto the altar as if she were the priest. Raskolnikov smiled in wonder. She took a ragged cloth from her pocket, unrolled it, and began rubbing and wiping the dark, engraved wooden pillar to the left of the altar, shining and shining it. When at last she had done with that one, she crossed to the other side, kneeling with difficulty in the middle on her way, and began on the opposite pillar. Raskolnikov followed her with his tired eyes as she went into the corner and began on the infinite task of the confessional box's intricate trellis. It was possible that she intended to clean the entire church from top to bottom. It would be the death of her, Raskolnikov thought, and if his friend Razumikhin were here no doubt he would jump to his feet and help her with the chore.

Enough.

He must leave. To hell with the weather.

Stiffly, he straightened his body and rose to his feet, wistfully gazing one final time at the peaceful altar and cross above it, and at the woman engrossed in her work. A little reluctantly, he walked around the back of the orderly pews in their calm, dark repose. He reacquainted himself with the bony handle of the hatchet and crossed the aisle, bending to genuflect out of old habit, and made his way to the door, the sudden movement filling his head with dizziness.

He passed out of the first pair of doors, then the second, and found himself face to face with the gusting rain once more. Without hesitation, he plunged into it, its rude pattering on the floor of the courtyard filling his ears, the wind changing its direction and pounding the left side of his face and his ear drums.

He hurried into the street and scanned it.

Nobody. Nothing.

He located her building, standing ugly and arrogant above the surrounding houses. Pushing himself through the storm, he gained on it quickly. Builders had abandoned their work in the yard outside. He hesitated in front of the looming block of apartments, blood thumping in his veins. He thought of the church.

He scurried towards the entrance and tried the door. Open. He slipped inside and up the stone stairs, but paused halfway up, water dripping like blood and collecting in a dark pool at his feet. His breathing wouldn't come regularly. He gasped and panted, as if he were choking on the awful act itself.

Just to the top, along a few doors, and knock. Once inside nothing could stop him. She would be bludgeoned to death with the back of the blade in return for her meanness. He wished it could be easier. If only the tranquillity of the church could preside. But he had the will to do this; his aim was noble and he was therefore morally exempt, unlike others.

Raskolnikov made an effort to breathe deeply, smoothly. Was this pain equal to the laboured steps of the woman in the church?

He stood there halfway up the staircase, frozen against the wall, for several minutes.

He could still smell the incense. Its scent was grey and velvet.

He turned in horror and staggered down the staircase, burst outside and rushed back the way he had come, the wind sweeping behind him.

Back through the rainswept streets without turning to look at the dreadful apartments one more time, past the church and the spot where he had fallen, as far as the murky green river. Still no-one here. He checked anyway, cautiously searching the misty swirl, took out the hatchet and hurled it into the depths of the stinking water, where it sank immediately. All he could see were the fleeting holes made by the striking rain in the surface of the river.

Raskolnikov crossed the bridge. The wind had dropped, but he had to hold onto the railing all the same. On the other side, he slowed his pace and took a different turning, into a narrow road full of overhanging, rickety houses.

At the end of the road was the tavern he sought. Hiding under the ledge that jutted into the street from the second storey sheltered a scrawny girl in dirty rags, just out of the way of the rain. Her eyes stared sorrowfully ahead, round and hungry. She didn't pay attention to Raskolnikov and seemed oblivious of the shouted conversations that came from inside, heard even above the storm.

For a moment he looked at her pale face, then heaved open the thick oak door of the inn.

Laughter and arguments, smoke and the smell of damp clothes greeted him.

Raskolnikov took a table in the gloomy corner and ordered a vodka.

Finding the Plot

Three o' clock: Temple by Day

Seya Ward, Yokohama

Maybe there will be some ghosts at the temple, ghosts clutching secret stories to their hearts that I can prize from them. A ghost story would do.

My room is cosy with the little heater whirring away, but a squawk from a crow interrupts my reverie. Another, from its companion, follows instantly. They are calling me to arms.

It's late afternoon now as I set off for the temple on the hill, in the exact opposite direction to the forest. I need a big, heavy coat even more now that it's getting so cold, and a hat and scarf are wise. As I approach the steep, sloping hill up to the temple I notice that the sun's quite high and the sky is cloudless.

I stride up the hill with resolve. I am, however, soon disappointed. There won't be ghosts here – or a story lying in plain sight.

I can't deny the beauty of the simple architecture with its curving roof, its raised platform, two-feet off the ground, wooden steps leading up to a gateway in front of the steps, wooden beams between white walls, criss-crossed wood concealing sliding doors into the inside of the temple.

Lanky, moss-covered trees bend this way and that near a stone wall and black, iron fence on top of the wall. A thick grove of bamboos, each with white hoops on their green stems, faces the temple wall and recedes downhill into the background. The cemetery beside the bamboos completes the scene.

But oddly, I feel like I shouldn't be here. It's not that any of the occasional passers-by turn their heads in my direction before hurrying on; they don't, and no-one questions my presence here. I just feel like an intruder, for some strange reason.

I notice washing poles and pegs standing to the right of the temple, a small, grey-roofed, wooden cottage to its left. There is an occasional passing car below in the street. Upturned dish-shaped baskets on the sacred outer walkway around the temple are a further sign of life. There is nowhere to sit, no way to pause here for a while.

In the corner of the temple grounds, there is another platform, made of stone and only three steps high. In its centre, a massive iron bell of dark grey hangs in between four new-looking wooden pillars. The grey roof curves like the temple's, but a smaller version. I perch on a corner of the outer wall, gazing at the thin road beyond. The underside of the bell platform's roof is decorated with intricate carvings, wooden decorations fanning outwards like chestnut brown rays of sunshine.

These surroundings should throw up a tale. The clear sky holds promise. Yet there is neither the stillness and solitude of a remote country temple, nor the hustle-bustle of a fully-fledged city scene. People go about their daily business, and it infringes on my space – as I encroach on theirs. I sit here writing notes and looking and feeling out this place, and I seem to be trespassing. I'm surprised nobody has come to chase me away.

Fittingly, a small man in a grey suit emerges from the temple cottage carrying a smart black case, and not long after, the postman draws up on an efficient red motorbike to deliver today's communication from the modern world outside. I go completely unnoticed; contrary to my unease, no-one minds me.

So much for mystery, intrigue and ghostliness at the temple.

There's no point in staying here. As I leave, I glance through the bamboo wood and notice that a dirty, rusted barbed wire fence deters entry. Not a metre in height, it would bar no-one from entering, but its presence is enough. Instead of obeying it, however, I climb easily over it and follow a tiny path that leads through the cemetery.

The stone shrines, decked out in rocks, flowers and miniature Buddhas are so much more pleasant than *traditional English gravestones, plunged into the ground like stakes into evil spirits. I would rather visit and remember my loved ones here and rest a little on a nearby tree stump than stand in a grim, dreary litter of graves on the ground.*

There is a strange, metallic casket standing in a clearing between some trees over on the far side of the cemetery. It sends a shiver rocketing down my spine. An uncomfortable feeling comes over me when I look at it. I don't know why. Perhaps it stands for something, something more than just the cycle of change, of birth and death and rebirth.

Soon I emerge from the trees onto the main road again. I'm anonymous in the crowded street, unlike in the grounds of the temple.

If I could steal away to the temple at night, and somehow open the forbidding doors, and lie on the floor so that I couldn't be seen from outside, I'm almost sure that a great story would be easy to find, and I could prostrate myself there determinedly penning it at my leisure.

I hadn't 52ealized it but my hands are cold right through. I thrust them in my coat pockets and go back home.

The Coffin: Prelude

Screaming was worse.

Like howling into his own face. The strangled shouts reverberating and clattering around the inside of the coffin.

He shut his mouth. Struggling instead for normal breaths from the thick air.

Tried to think.

Strained to remember: what he had done the day before; where he had been; who he was.

Fragmented images. Colours and shades. Odd words of conversation. These only.

His memory seized hold of something complete and moved faster and faster with it: going to bed – presumably a few hours before. Coming home from the office at ten, later than usual. Eating and watching TV – could see the suntanned, grinning face of the game show presenter right now, the comical expressions of contestants as they tried ever so hard to please, tried to win money and fame, could hear the rising pitch of audience laughter. Something else on the TV – had it been a programme on the TV, or was it a book he'd been reading before he'd slept – the main character falling, falling, falling into the abyss…? Before that, a long day's work and two and a half beers with his colleagues. Tomorrow was Friday. Drinking until late. Needed to sleep well tonight to have plenty of energy. Brushing his teeth, changing into pyjamas, checking the alarm clock.

Now here.

How?

Heart pound-pound-pounding, he reached out his hands above him once again. Pushed. Nothing moved. A bead of sweat rolled from his forehead down the side of his scalp. A moment of anger: he kicked the lid. It sent a numbing pain through his foot.

Not a dream.

"Am I fucking dead?" He laughed like a madman. "That would explain it. ...I don't feel dead."

He could feel the pendant he wore lying on his chest, its metal warm against his body. He was wearing clothes. He could feel their soaked cloth sticking to him.

No sound apart from his own laboured breathing. An infinity of ugly silence rushing and tearing at him like a waterfall until he imagined sounds – footsteps nearby, and a scoff of laughter echoing in his head. Maybe he was deaf now, too.

Minutes idled by like hours.

Was this life after death, lying here in this box for eternity? Was it possible to die again, having already died once? He tried the lid with no result. Another shudder passed through him.

In spite of himself, he began to grow accustomed to his new environment. No choice.

He pushed again, out of petrified instinct.

Movement.

The roof above had moved.

Gravity wrenched its weight back down on him, but he summoned the strength that hadn't been drained away and heaved upwards. Still disbelieving, he saw the lid remain open, protruding into the sky on the right-hand side of the coffin.

He scrambled out like a lunatic.

Tried to get his bearings, eyes adjusting to the new shade of blackness. A baby released with uncertainty into the psychedelia of new life. A yellow half-moon gave hazy light to the cloudless sky.

He wanted to run as fast as he could but an urge possessed him to remain.

Vision now accustomed to the dark, he scrutinized the enclosed area about him. Surrounded by trees. The coffin stood on a slope covered with thick grass and weeds. Silhouettes less than half his height also littered the gentle hill. What were those black shapes?

Headstones.

His coffin didn't have a headstone.

The faint drone of traffic occasionally shooting by somewhere in the distance. A warm night – but shivering, he stepped closer to the side of the coffin. The dry earth caressed his bare feet.

There was nothing unexpected on the inside of the coffin.

He looked in both directions, up and down the hill. Didn't know where he was or which way to go. In panic, he hurried upwards. From the top of the slope, he could see a few dilapidated houses on the other side of the hill. A wall of trees behind him. And a concrete path ahead, winding around the corner and out of sight. The traffic noise was louder up here.

Then he spotted something he recognised.

Small in the distance, a square of neon red light. He tried to place it and it came to him: the Riverside Hotel.

Swamped with relief and equally dumbfounded, he realised he wasn't far from home. The landscape below began to fall into place. In the darkness, he made out the familiar outlines of the restaurants next to the road.

Gravel biting at his feet, he made his way down the path and rounded the corner at the bottom of the hill. Out of nowhere a dog began barking furiously at him, accusing, its burly silhouette just about restrained by a weak-looking rope tied to its kennel. He kept walking. Once the dog was left behind, its din stopped abruptly.

Crossed the main road. Into the dark back street leading all the way to his block of flats. Up the iron steps to his front door and inside.

The first thing he did was grab his alarm clock from beside the bed – the bed that he had climbed safely into earlier in the night. The luminous green digital figures said 'three-thirty'. He put his head in his hands in torment, thinking it highly possible he had gone mad.

He had to reason this out. He stood in a pool of fear under the yellow light in the small living room, unable to think clearly.

He put down the clock and went into the next room, where there was a full-length mirror. Peered at his face in the dusty glass. It didn't tell him anything. His throat was dry and he went into the kitchen to get a glass of water. On second thoughts, he unscrewed the cap of the brandy bottle and poured himself a generous glassful.

He craved sleep. It was coming closer and there was nothing he could do to fight it.

At least in sleep, there was respite from reality.

In his sleep, he dreamt with hallucinogenic clarity of being in a crowded pub with old friends from schooldays. He wanted to find Sue, a good friend from that period of his life – curt and something of a loner but generous-hearted.

Somebody said she was upstairs. Upstairs he went. Found a roof garden, high above the smoke and stench of the frantic city. He scoured the faces of the people there, but couldn't find her, although one young woman bore a resemblance. He'd never seen this woman but, as in dreams, was able to guess that she must be Sue's sister: the same dark yet compassionate expression, frowning heavy eyebrows. She in turn gazed at him with a beautiful even smile and quick, understanding blue eyes.

"I'm Nat. Do you know where Sue is?"

Her eyes widened as she realised who he was. She threw her arms around him, giving him the tightest, most loving embrace he had ever received. He had no idea why she was so happy to see him, or why she held him as if he must never go away, but the sensation was warm and beautiful; her emotion seeped into him.

Nat woke up with the dream drawing a heavy mist over his mind. He spent ten minutes without stirring, endeavouring to relive the perfect embrace. Something about being held in those passionate arms made sense, even though the dream itself didn't appear to.

Well, we all we want to be loved, don't we? He considered.

Nat managed to put his consternation the back of his mind the following day and convince himself that nothing had happened. He knew better but was gallant in his denial.

A routine Friday night, they stumbled through a drunken fog and collided with football talk, impotent anger about politics and, as the beers they had been pouring down took full effect, lustful idolization of women. A normal Friday night.

Through the haze of alcohol, Nat was vaguely surprised that he could dismiss so efficiently the unease that was gnawing on his brain, that he could so easily continue old habits. He used each beer like a bar of soap to wash away the more urgent matter that he knew he ought to be addressing. The unfolding night reassured him of his own normality.

They were talking about a colleague in the office, a solicitor who never socialised, rarely spoke except to clients, but was rumoured to be something of a legal genius. He was infamous for ducking into his office at the sight of anyone approaching him to make friendly conversation.

"He's one strange guy all right," Nat said.

"He's probably a serial killer in his free time," Jeremy remarked. "You never know."

"Or else he's just a sad case, plain and simple," Paul corrected him.

Nat laughed. "I swear he actually did hide from me the other day. He ducked into an empty office as I was coming. Most peculiar."

"But what's he do when he's not working?" Paul asked in some confusion.

Jeremy looked at him. "I told you."

Paul shook his head. "I don't know about anything as sinister as that. He probably still lives with his grandmother."

For a moment, Nat considered putting Paul right on that comment. Nat had grown up with his grandmother – Paul knew that. He let it pass. He certainly didn't want to put himself in the same category as the colleague they were disparaging.

A thin wave of silvery-blue smoke snaked its way across the table causing Nat to turn absently and find its source. Behind him a group of five young office workers were huddled around their own table, deep in discussion. The smoker had his back to Nat and was listening intently to the animated explanation of a grinning woman with short, blonde hair and a brightly-painted, full red mouth. Impossible to hear what they were saying, all sound mutated and drowned out by the rumble of a hundred people talking at the same time, glasses scraping and thumping on tables. He watched her red lips and it occurred to Nat that she was chatting underwater, they were all underwater. Noticing him looking her way, she flashed him a look of nervous suspicion, but carried on her conversation in the safety of her group of friends.

"Nat? Are you still with us, Nat?" It was Paul's voice calling him back from reverie.

Nat returned his attention to the familiar face, shiny glasses and cheerful tie of his colleague.

"Sorry."

Nat studied the two colleagues sitting across the pool of white light that sprayed out from above the table. Other tables looked to be under less of a glare, and Nat eyed the scattered bunches of drinkers, most of whom were smartly suited like themselves, and most of them standing, as they chattered and laughed in the midst of clouds of smoke and dim light.

By closing time, Jeremy and Paul were just getting warmed up, hatching plans for a progression to one or another of the city's many nightclubs, but Nat was feeling the force of the previous night's drama blended with all the alcohol. The evening had had a strange quality like thick mud, pulling him down into it as he struggled.

Having been turfed unceremoniously out of the pub, they argued the point in the car park, Nat's colleagues unwilling to accept his protests.

"Go on, guys, you go on. I've really had it for tonight." Nat grinned sheepishly.

"Oh, come on, Nat," Paul scolded him. "It's usually the other way around – you persuading me to go on somewhere else, drink more, not be so boring."

"No." Nat held up both hands to show his resolution. "Not tonight, guys."

Fifteen minutes later the three of them were buying a first drink in a nearby club, having been deposited after a short taxi ride and descended into the depths below street level. The deafening music pumped out reassuringly, throbbing in their alcohol-ridden blood, and shaking the floor with its pulsing bass and rattle of tinny syncopated drum and cymbal sounds. Lights flashing and careening off walls, across the dance floor. Virtually naked professional dancers gyrating on raised platforms and sliding predictably up and down against steel poles.

Jeremy led the way through crowds of revellers squashed together at the edge of the brighter dancing area – a pool of shuffling bodies and bobbing serious faces that ignored them as they squeezed apologetically through. He located a small enclave for relaxing, away from the action.

With the blend of fatigue and booze, Nat's control over his words and movements was sliding further away from him now, but a new lease of life had arrived from some hidden reserve of adrenalin. Against his better, more sober judgement, he was gripped by the urge to confide in his two colleagues about the previous night's plight. But as he was juggling with the idea, Paul got up abruptly, speaking inaudibly against the music, and began to dance again, throwing his body around like a lunatic in his own incomparable style. Was it evocative of the inner workings of his mind – all happy foolery, the wise village idiot? Or was this jazziness just the toy of alcohol, concealing the serious and responsible professional.

Jeremy and Nat watched and laughed, yelling encouragement from time to time. Then they were alone, masked by the darkness of their cubicle. Nat glanced at the silver table, curved like a misshapen pear, with its embedded sparkling jewels, and then across at his counterpart, conscious of a sudden wave of sobriety. Should he tell Jeremy that he had gone to bed the night before only to wake up in a coffin, trapped? At long last escaping into the night air to make his way home in pyjamas?

He respected his colleague. On several occasions, Nat had seen evidence of Jeremy jumping to help people, despite the brash exterior he liked to keep in place. He had gone out of his way to make Nat feel welcome when he had first joined the company.

But this would be the biggest joke of the century.

Even if it was taken seriously, that might be worse. His sanity would be questioned.

An ample-breasted woman in a shiny blue miniskirt walked languidly past them. Nat put his odd story to the back of his mind once more. This was a world far removed from reality; Nat could be another person here, forget all troubles.

He resumed a yelled conversation with Jeremy interspersed with several puzzled Whats? And Pardons? As they battled with the volume of the music. Jeremy, he noticed, kept his comments to economical, shouted sentences, blue eyes scanning the assortment of people floating past, and Nat endeavoured to copy the expert in an effort to save his flagging energy.

His eyelids were growing heavy, and he had to resort to frequent trips to the crowded bar in order to keep them open. Their drinks became shorter and more colourful, bright greens and blues, like the reeling, flickering lights. When his forlorn gaze followed a particularly attractive figure or a sympathetic-looking face, Nat made his way to the action and danced nearby for a while, employing what he hoped were passable moves.

At two o' clock, Paul was finally ready to leave and Nat, who might usually have stayed longer, decided to go with him. They emerged from the depths of the club into the deserted street.

A piece of newspaper danced along the pavement ahead of them as they walked.

"Are you all right?" Paul inquired, intuitive as usual.

So he had noticed that something wasn't right.

"No, no. Yeah. I'm fine. Just a bit more tired than normal. I didn't sleep very well last night, that's all."

"Mm, okay. You seem slightly... I don't know... distracted." Despite all they had drunk, his tone was that of a doctor calmly inviting a patient to confide in him, but Nat had resolved not to mention anything by now.

"No. I'm fine," he smiled. It bothered him that Paul could detect that something was wrong so easily.

They took a taxi, and Paul got out first, leaving Nat to fight to stay awake for the rest of the journey.

At last he stumbled home, unlocked his front door which he felt like he hadn't seen for a week, and crashed into bed after two minutes, barely stopping to shove a toothbrush around his mouth at high-speed.

He slept in the deep cloudy waters of drunkenness, waking up at exactly midday.

Upon returning to consciousness, he told himself blearily that he was twenty-nine years old and really should be spending his weekends more productively. The sun was wrestling with the lime green curtains, spilling one determined ray of light across the carpet. He lay there, trying to put back together the fragments of the night before. Had he given away something that he hadn't meant to? He gave up and let it all rattle around in the back of his dizzy head.

He was bitten into com'lete wakefulness by the realisation that his sleep had been
    undisturbed.

"Thank God," he said in triumph.

Had that Thursday been a one-off? Had it happened at all?

Grimacing uneasily as he remembered it, he decided that he had been working too hard. He had been under a lot of stress. He needed to unwind. His eyes fell on a book on the floor, Interview with the Vampire. He must have been reading it for at least three months and he wasn't halfway through yet. He reached out of bed and picked it up, and spent a further hour lazily reading the rolling, poetic lines, conscious of the irony of reading horror given his own real concerns about the night before last. Then, noticing how insistently his stomach was rumbling, he threw on some clothes and traipsed down the street towards the burger shop.

This took him quite near to Thursday night's site of horror. His hunger evaporated.

He knew that he ought to go back up the hill and check if the coffin was there or not. Part of him wanted just to forget it – to bury it in his mind, if not in the earth.

But he turned into the back-street and climbed the steep slope until he was at the top of the dreadful hill. He didn't allow himself to hesitate for fear that he would change his mind, and turned left, away from the thick forest ahead and into the more thinly tree-covered grove where, dotted here and there, he spotted the unsavoury shapes of tombstones.

Looking down this second slope, he saw it: the rectangular box of plain metal that he had inhabited, the unburied coffin.

He turned and threw up the contents of his stomach, exorcising the stupid drinks of the previous night, the superficial mirth and the garish energy. He spewed and retched, splashing the leaves. He was all too conscious that he had to stop doing this so often.

Panting, and wiping his mouth, he hurried off down the slope. Perhaps he should have told someone about it but now he was going to pursue a policy of firm denial. Ignorance was bliss.

Finding the Plot

Four o' clock: City by Day

Tokyo City

I certainly couldn't think clearly at the temple. I couldn't even relax. I could hardly breathe.

I head towards the station now. Big steel boxes take all the people, packed like fish, to the bright lights. It's a little ironic that I need a capital city in which to feel untroubled by the peering hundreds of eyes around me, but there you have it.

Snow is wisping down in tiny, lonely crumbs, each one doing its own thing. It doesn't settle on the ground, but disappears instantly as if it never was. Some crows play about in a distant, bony tree, which makes me think of the forest. An unusual, long-legged, graceful white bird joins them, standing on a pile of earth at the base of the tree, looking out-of-place, and belonging surely to a quiet, rippling lake or marsh, but a crow soon puts it in its place by chasing it away.

What does the big city hold in store?

When I arrive, the snow is swirling around and around as it descends and clings to my bulky coat, speckling the dark blue with little pieces of white. As I leave the station behind, it's beginning to cover the pavements and occasional bits of greenery at the edge of the pavement. A little fountain overflows desperately into its pond with the sudden rush of new water.

I take a camera film (with my pictures of the forest and temple) into a shop to be developed and the cashier faces me as if he's seen a ghost, but in doing so he looks like a ghost himself. What's wrong with him? *I wonder. Every encounter with shop workers in the city is a trial. They bark at you and send you on your way. Undeterred, I seek a coffee shop with enough space to sit undisturbed and watch life rush past me.*

I enter a I and order a cup of tea from a cashier. She is pleasant – albeit without seeming to hear me properly the first and second times that I spoke. She looks shell-shocked by what I say. Perhaps she is nervous or shy, or suffering from some kind of malady. She provides me with just a tea bag in a packet and a cup of hot water. The customer must make their own tea by the look of it. There aren't any vacant window seats and I settle for a corner seat. Putting my coat on the back of my chair, I glance around at the four o' clock men who drink their coffees and teas with stony faces.

Blocking out the incessant race-track commentary voices to my right as they go up and down, up and down, with their startling tales of clocks, minutes and schedules – something is very unfair, apparently – I drape the sorry-looking tea bag over the cup's lid, take a sip, and am relieved at how reassuring a poor cup of tea can taste when you're thirsty and cold enough.

Through the window, down below, people scamper along the pavement underneath their tilted umbrellas. It's a weary journey up a city street in the snow and in the four o' clock heaviness. Judging by the sour faces and the bitter, complaining voices around me, it's a weary business sitting in a tea shop, as well. I hunch over my hot drink. I don't let myself get too comfortable.

The place Is sterile and It's not long before I return my tray and prepare to float back out into the trudging masses. It's hectic outside, in the heart of the city – the insane centre that hums like one giant, out-of-control animal made of millions of people. A grey bus blocks my view for a few minutes, then departs belching black-grey, filthy clouds. The road slopes to my left and away out of sight. It's grey too, along with the nearby buildings and supermarket opposite.

I stand still, absorbing life. So many people pass rapidly to my left and right on the pavement that they become caught up in one continuous blur. Like a revolving wheel, they aren't still for long enough to make out who or what they really are and where they might, perhaps, be going.

Men in perfect suits. Shapeless women with handbags and shopping bags. Young couples in jeans and mini-skirts. The older women have the biggest coats. The groceries make their way home. People wait facelessly, inoffensively at the bus stop. Kids walk faster and not in a straight line. A mother takes her boy into a restaurant. A cake box is forlornly carried past my frame of sight. Some of them catch a glimpse of me and stare back. I could swear I saw some sort of zombie caught up in one throng of hurrying pedestrians, at the very least a half-zombie, half-man. His face wasn't quite right, he lurched, but was gone in the blink of an eye.

On and on it goes. I don't think it ever stops. It's all very real, but it's hard to discern any precise story behind each image. I can only wonder. After some time, sad as I am to say, it all becomes part of the same thing. Another bus. Another face. The buildings.

I'm sure there used to be a time when all of this movement and chaos felt alive to me, and I was part of it. Weren't the colours brighter and the faces more distinct, every passing moment containing a small joy within? Catching a bus just in time, a small child's laugh – they were filled with wonder. Now I'm beholding it all with a strange detachment and calm, almost as though I'm not really here.

Time to go. Still storyless.

City Man 1, City Man 2

Zoo-Man

It was at the zoo that it happened, of all places. He had just stopped at the lions. There they were, docile and bored, two of them slumped on the floor like house cats, pets waiting for the appointed hour of food, a stroke and some TV programmes. House cats love TV; it's so relaxing.

One of the lions at the back of the prison paced restlessly up and down. His tail twitched. There was an angry grimace on his face that shouldn't be allowed to startle the customers, just titillate them.

John stopped outside the lions' house and hardly had a chance to take them in before there was a twitching at his eye. An annoying twitching. He tried to rub it away, gently at first, massaging his eye, then rubbing it harder, harder, turning into a furious tearing at his socket. Too much coffee, he reflected quickly.

Our home, your coffee. Because we love you.

That slogan was jammed in his head.

How many stamps were there on his points card? There were six. He had passed the point of no return.

"John!" someone called. He turned. He was here alone. Who was calling? "Hel-lo!"

He looked around, still clawing at his eye. A woman with long, blonde hair ran up and embraced a handsome fellow in a light grey suit. A handsome guy presumably called John, like him.

The news was in his head. Three-year old ruthlessly snatched from his parents. The suntanned, grinning (hiding his grin) news presenter, feigning some sort of aggressive compassion, some sort of forced horror, a sombre game show host. Photo of the snatched toddler. Tanks rolled into a Middle Eastern country. Suited politicians looked overweight and overpaid in the studio as they passed judgement. Commercials ran. Bouncing breasts advertised toothpaste. Whiter than white. Shining sparkling happy joy. Then Victoria and Alvaro Tavella appeared, weeping and worrying.

"Could be dead," said the news reader.

And his eye was sitting uncomfortably in its socket. Our home, your coffee had made his eye freak out. People in the office arguing. The corpse in the corner, the Marketing Manager, oversaw all and occasionally she said, "We need to squeeze more money out of the clients, that's what we need to do." And then she brushed grave soil from out of her dead, scraggy hair. "We need a new form, too. This one isn't methodical enough."

"Yes, good point," he would typically agree.

But now blood was screaming through his head. His thoughts wouldn't slow down. He couldn't think but he couldn't stop thinking. And he could not control the tick in his eye, or was it a cross? Cross with you, his mother had said, her face boiling like a red lobster.

He stood over the milk, flowing into the carpet, there to stink for weeks. But it made your teeth whiter than white, or your bones stronger than strong. Thank you, cows, for your involuntary gift.

He sank to his knees. The other john was on his mobile phone and looked curiously in this John's direction, then carried on with his mobile conversation. He clutched his head in his hands. His face was a lobster in the pot. People were coming to look now, a spectacle more exciting and concerning than lions and three-year olds. News and money, the elephants, the spider house, a rush of traffic and electric lights pouring incessantly through his head, brain frying up like a nice egg in the pan, the sound was the last thing he was conscious of: a high-pitched screaming sound cutting his brain in two, right and left hemisphere, schizophrenia and manic depression.

He must have slumped to the floor. The last thing was a brief dream, a peaceful moment, all perfectly still, a mirror, a horizontal mirror, in fact the ocean gone flat, in fact he was the ocean, very peculiar...

Zom-Man

I'll be walking along near the Thames, oblivious to the bloated dead bodies all murdered and head-beaten lying down there at the bottom getting chewed up by cancerous fishes, who complain to each other in fish signals about the deteriorating quality of the river water. Too right.

And as I'm walking along, in search of coffee, I will know that, apart from not knowing where I am going, or what I am searching for, because I've forgotten temporarily until some new stimulus arrives, walking along anyway when someone barges into me, hurrying a bit faster than me.

It won't hurt but it will annoy me because things annoy you when you're in the city, claustrophobed together with millions of other hurriers, some full of purpose and knowing why they're hurrying, others just hurrying because they don't want to break with the etiquette of the city.

I'll look up to see who's bumped into me, silently cursing him or her but extra-silently in case it's some mad fucker. And sure enough, it will be a mad-looking fucker who has barged past. I'll watch him surreptitiously in case he sees me and gets angry but he'll be gone, lost in his own hurries. The guy will look around him unseeingly, his dirty white shirt untucked and flapping with his hurry-harry. His grey hair will be unbrushed, his arms will flail, he'll take a couple more pedestrians with him as he sweeps past like a tumbleweed.

He'll be uttering half-words that sound like bits of news or a conversation half-remembered. It will sound like a horrible mantra:

"In heaven… in heaven…"

On and on, to himself. He'll be out of control, yellow froth foaming at his grey lips.

Or is he muttering,

"Sin heaven"? …Or, "In seven?"

It's difficult to make out.

Fittingly, it will be outside a museum celebrating torture and murder in London's past that this will happen.

Later, I will look back and think how he was a bit like a zombie. I'll call him a Zom-Man. There are many such zombies in the city. Not even metaphorically. They seem slightly to have relinquished their grip on life, one foot somewhere unpleasant far below, their minds unable to resist the dark depths of unnecessary detail they have encountered somewhere along the line.

It'll be here that it all tips, and tips, and slides downhill. And there won't be anything you can do about it. Apart from write it all down.

Will there?

So I'll continue on to the *Missing Bean*, order a cappuccino with almond milk, and bemoan that it doesn't froth in quite the same way as regular milk.

I'll peer into the cup for clues and, with concern, see the froth is yellowish and the coffee a deathly grey colour.

Finding the Plot

Five o' clock: Reflections

Nowhere, Somewhere

The melancholy five o'clock dusk is a time for reflections. The bitterly cold darkness envelops all of the light. Day is fading from existence …for today.

I found the city view that I wanted, the land of adverts several metres high, TV clips while you wait to cross, monstrous buildings. A thousand impenetrable stories streaming by.

And still I didn't find a story to tell.

I contemplate whether I'm the one moving through this city or if I'm just watching from the outside, unseen, like something forgotten. I start to wonder if it's all just a matter of company. Do I feel isolated because I don't have anyone to think aloud to, some kind of comrade-in-plot? A story needs characters.

The Friend

The electric buzz of the doorbell jerked Rachel from her reverie. She was debating with herself whether or not to answer it when it gave out a second low-pitched screech.

She dragged herself from her slumped position on the couch, not really wanting to leave the cartoon she'd been watching, glanced in the mirror to ruffle her hair into a slightly better mess and stood in front of the door. It wasn't exactly early so she wondered who it could be. Not a friend or someone from the salon. No, nobody'd been round lately.

Belatedly she swung open the door and gazed uncertainly at the shape of a person in front of her. A youngish, attractive woman, well-dressed, with a friendly smile and only a hint of shyness. Her red coat was damp about the shoulders from the rain outside and an umbrella dripped onto the stone floor in the corridor outside the flat.

Rachel didn't say anything, waiting for the stranger to speak first. She did look familiar somehow. A customer perhaps. Rachel tried to look a shade less hostile, just in case. The woman simply carried on smiling radiantly until it dawned on Rachel that she was waiting to be recognized.

Rachel was careful to use her polite, well-spoken voice. "I'm sorry. Do I know you?"

"Rachel, you don't recognize me, do you?" The stranger didn't seem to mind, anyway.

"Er, no..."

"It's me... Isabelle."

Had the woman made a mistake? Rachel didn't know anyone called that, not that she could remember anyway. Although it did ring a bell...

"I know. It's been a hell of a long time. But you haven't changed all that much. I didn't think had. Then again, we were very young."

Rachel frantically searched her memory. She didn't really want to know, but who on earth...?

The only time she'd ever known someone called Isabelle had indeed been when she'd been very young, but this wasn't her. That Isabelle had been a figment of dreams, a childhood companion who had inhabited Rachel's imagination. At the same time, she found herself double-taking: she had been an imaginary friend, hadn't she? Of course she had, so that wasn't the answer.

"I think you've made a..." The woman had already used her name, so it wasn't a mistake.

"I'm sorry. I can't remember you."

The woman was unperturbed, still smiling. She had nice white teeth, lots of them.

"We were friends when we were so young. I haven't seen you since we were five."

"Look. I really don't know anyone called Isabelle. I'm terribly sorry. I don't know how you know my name, but if you will excuse me, it's rather late..."

"Hill Head? Hill Head, Rachel," she said eagerly, smiling less widely but undaunted, sure that Rachel would catch on any minute now. She didn't see the look of horror that swept across her face. "We played on the beach, by the sea – especially in the Summer. Together every day."

She laughed. "You used to blame me when you did something wrong."

Rachel reached out for the doorway, her legs weak. A slight dizziness came over her but with an effort she fought it off. Now she knew who this woman purported to be, but that was impossible. That Isabelle hadn't been real. But neither could this be an imposter standing before her because no-one had known of her.

"Isabelle?" she said hesitantly.

"Yes." The woman looked pleased. "Well I thought I'd pay you a visit after all this time. It wasn't easy to track you down, but then it wasn't so hard either." She paused. "Can I come in... or have I caught you at a bad time?"

Let her in? The woman was either a ghost or a trickster. Rachel considered slamming the door shut and pouring herself a generous Scotch. And yet, something about Isabelle was compelling. For an instant, she wanted to believe in her. After all, here she was, in flesh and blood, calling herself by the right name. Even if it was only to get to the bottom of the matter, she stood back and gestured for her to come in, only regretting the chaotic state of her home – it looked like she had been robbed – when the smart woman had already confidently entered and stood in the hall between the kitchen and the living room.

"Er, yes, come in, I mean go in – to the living room." Rachel pointed a flustered finger at the room on the right. There wasn't anything she could do now about the work clothes strewn across the floor, the open drawers with their contents all over the place, the collection of dirty cups and plates, or the sinister-looking bottle of whisky that had been keeping her company on the couch.

"Do you want a drink?"

"I'd love one."

Isabelle, if that was her name, hadn't pulled a disgusted face at the clutter of the room anyway.

"Sit anywhere you like. It's a bit of a mess." Rachel laughed self-consciously.

Isabelle took the seat that Rachel had vacated when she'd answered the door. She sat upright on the edge of the sofa as though she didn't want to be rude by getting too comfortable. Yet at the same time she looked completely at ease. Rachel escaped into the kitchen, unable to make sense of this strange visit. Only then did she remember that she hadn't asked her guest what she wanted to drink.

Through the steam of her mug of coffee, Rachel examined her visitor. Her even smile was her most distinctive feature, unashamedly showing two rows of even teeth. There wasn't any deceit hidden in it, not that Rachel could detect anyway, and her eyes shone with energy and enthusiasm. Her fair hair had changed little in colour since childhood – or Rachel's memory of it. Now it was cut just above her shoulders, all one length. It suited her: smart but feminine.

The same was true of the light grey suit she wore, professional but not dull.

Realizing that Isabelle was studying her too, Rachel stared into the hot black liquid inside her cup. "God, it's been so long," the stranger said. "I didn't know what to expect."

Rachel gave her a suspicious glance.

"What are you doing these days, Rachel?"

"I... well I'm a hair stylist." She wondered how this would sound to her sophisticated-looking guest.

"Oh." Isabelle nodded.

"And I run a salon and teach hairdressing sometimes."

"Sounds interesting. I teach too." Rachel sipped her coffee and listened warily. "I'm a lecturer... philosophy. Serious stuff." She raised her eyebrows in self-mockery.

Over their coffee, Isabelle talked at length about her life since they had parted company. She had gone to school in Portsmouth and then university in Cambridge where she had studied philosophy. She'd had her share of boyfriends, of vodka drinking competitions and of games of summer tennis, it seemed. Now she was lecturing at the University of Durham. By all appearances, life had smiled on her; not only did she have a good career but she looked happy and confident. She was in control of her life, Rachel concluded. But all the while she listened, even when she couldn't help laughing at the way Isabelle told a tale with wide, honest blue eyes, Rachel knew that this was all wrong. This woman could not be who she said she was.

Though she spoke of the village they had grown up in and knew Portsmouth and Southampton well enough, it simply wasn't possible. Despite this, they carried on talking over a second coffee. And then, reluctantly, it was Rachel's turn to say something about herself.

She told Isabelle about the salon, how she had risen to become the manager, that she found the work less enthralling than she had used to. She'd been busy recently. Not much chance to go out, do things, see people. Then she manoeuvred the conversation skilfully back to her guest, stopping short of telling her about her daughter, her marriage, her ex-husband. It was ludicrous enough to be chatting on with someone who wasn't supposed to exist. She wasn't about to pour forth the gory details of her private life. That would be too much.

There came a lull in the conversation. Isabelle looked contentedly around the room, her eyes resting briefly on the picture on the mantelpiece of a small girl grinning mischievously up from the beach, a blue sea gently rolling in behind her, a yellow blow-up bed floating near the shore and behind that a younger, less careworn Rachel in bikini emerging from the water. Rachel waited for the question that was bound to follow, but instead Isabelle collected herself and said:

"I should go. I'm sure you've got lots to do and I've taken enough of your time."

"Well... no..." Rachel faltered. "I enjoyed it." Inside she kicked herself. What was she saying? She had liked talking to someone who couldn't exist?

Isabelle picked up her cup to take it to the kitchen and Rachel intercepted, not wanting her to see the mess there as well.

"I'm staying with my sister tonight in the centre of town, but it'd be nice if we can meet again."

"You have a sister?"

"Uh huh." Isabelle looked at Rachel with puzzlement as if to question why she shouldn't have a sister. Not for the first time, Rachel was tempted to confront her. Who was she really?

What did she want? She would tell her that she couldn't be who she claimed.

Not knowing why, she resisted the urge and found herself ridiculously agreeing to meet for lunch in two days' time.

When Isabelle had left, gliding out of the building with the same pleasant self-assuredness with which she had arrived, Rachel hurried back inside the flat and, like a schoolgirl, spied on her guest as she gradually disappeared up the street and around the corner. She turned back to face the empty room. Now it was as before. The impossible Isabelle might never have existed. Rachel was all alone. The indentation on the sofa could have been her own. The clutter of the room was undisturbed. The clutter of her mind could return to its dreamy brooding. But a pleasant smell made a soft imprint on the room – the scent of milky white flowers. That much was different. It was a scent that Rachel didn't recognize, sweet without being sickly, bold but not overbearing. Isabelle had been in the room with her all right. There was no denying it.

Still Rachel went through to the kitchen, needing more proof. Two cups, side by side at the edge of the sink. Just like in childhood – two cups, one for Rachel and one for her secret friend Isabelle. And one of the cups had a faint trace of red lipstick on the rim – not Rachel's.

Rachel sensed a chill creep up her spine. What on earth had she been doing, talking to this imposter? – for that was the only thing that she could be. She had been such a fool to go along with the charade. Admittedly the whole business had taken her by surprise, but she ought to have pulled herself together and got rid of the woman, however charming and seemingly innocent. The bizarre thing was that Rachel had no idea how the intruder had got hold of the knowledge she had. There was no way that she could have plumbed the depths of Rachel's mind and located a hidden detail of her childhood. Ridiculous.

Even more surprising was that Rachel knew that she would go through with the next meeting.

She was looking forward to seeing Isabelle again, whoever she was. If any other old friend had come calling, she wouldn't have wanted to see them. Perhaps the mystery of an imaginary friend was enticing.

She forced herself to put it all from her mind and stared at the TV for a while without really watching it, had a stiff whisky and went to bed. Work the next day. There wasn't anything she could figure out about her curious visitor until they met again.

That night she dreamt that she was a small girl again, running along the deserted beach with her quiet, easygoing friend, safe from the dark, rough waves that chopped restlessly on the sea, a bright red kite fluttering merrily overhead against the deep blue sky.

When Isabelle waved at her from a table inside the I, it seemed as if they were two ordinary old friends meeting for lunch. She pushed the door open with some trepidation but she had steeled herself for the appointment and was determined not to be daunted by the peculiar occasion. Why should she be? She was the normal one, the one who existed.

As it was, Isabelle took the butterflies out of Rachel's stomach by chatting on as though they had never been out of each other's company.

"I got a coffee. I didn't wait. I need something to do while I wait for someone to turn up."

"Sure."

"This area's so nice. I think you're really lucky to live here, not in one of the gloomier parts of London."

"Yeah, I suppose it's all right."

"It's nice. Get yourself a drink. We've got so much to talk about."

Rachel wasn't at all sure that they had but could hardly argue with those flashing eyes and open smile. She ordered a black coffee from the pleasant middle-aged lady behind the counter and a small sandwich for the sake of making it through the working day. Then she was face to face with her new acquaintance. She looked nice again, dressed in less formal clothes than before, a tight orange top with a black velvet waistcoat over it. Rachel was surprised to see that she smoked. The crumpled remains of a cigarette in the ash tray might have belonged to someone else but not the plastic blue lighter that lay close to her pale hand on the table.

"Isn't this a nice place?" Isabelle whispered, leaning across the table.

"Yes. I haven't been here before actually." Rachel studied the pictures of brightly coloured fish on the orange walls. Despite the vivid colours, its atmosphere was restful, perhaps on account of the dark blue wooden beams and doorway and the soft lighting. In the glass cabinet nearby were all sorts of sandwich fillings: meat, tuna, salad, cheeses. She 78ealized that she had something of an appetite, after all.

She looked at Isabelle evenly. "How's your sister?"

"Oh, she's fine. Absolutely fine. We don't see as much of each other as we'd like, obviously, with me living at the opposite end of the country now." She hadn't hesitated to answer and it sounded convincing enough.

"I don't think I ever met her."

"Well she was six years older than us. I guess she always had her own things to do."

"I guess so."

"And how's your day going?" Isabelle asked levelly.

Rachel shrugged. "It's going." She smiled, not wanting to be a complete misery.

Isabelle frowned understandingly. "Soon be the weekend."

"Yeah. How long are you staying in this part of the world?"

"That's a good question. I'm on a kind of conference holiday, you could call it. I have some seminars to attend in relation to my work. I have to go out with the usual boring philosophy crowd afterwards, eat at overpriced restaurants, you know."

"Not really."

"Then you're not missing much. I prefer eating cheap with friends. Anyway, that takes up the whole day but I'm free at the weekend. I thought we could get together."

"Maybe," Rachel said noncommittally. The sandwich arrived along with the coffee and a brief friendly smile.

"Well I'll definitely be around this weekend, so if you want to do something..." Before Rachel could answer, Isabelle broke off in a different direction. "It's really good, you know. I don't think we've changed since we were five."

Rachel laughed. "You don't think so?"

"Yes, I often think that about myself, but I didn't expect it to be so easy to pick up our friendship where we left it. I only came to see you out of curiosity."

"I think I've changed an awful lot." Rachel remembered her ex-family and, forgetting the present, her thoughts spiralled to the bottom of the thick coffee.

When she caught Isabelle's eye again, she had the impression that her thoughts were easy to read, as though their friendship truly hadn't changed since childhood.

"Why do you think that?"

Rachel didn't want to talk about it but couldn't think of a way out of the subject. She looked at Isabelle squarely. "Have you had any children?"

"No!" She looked shocked, as though she had never considered the idea.

Rachel gritted her teeth. "It changes you, especially when you can't be with them."

Now she wished that she hadn't said anything, but Isabelle nodded sympathetically. Then she lit a cigarette, inhaling as if she had been starved of air until that moment.

"Sounds hard."

There was a pause. A thin stream of silky smoke left Isabelle's lips and rose towards the ceiling. Rachel sought answers in the depths of her coffee again.

"It's a depressing subject. But that's why I think I've changed, since you ask. Let's talk about something else."

"Okay." Isabelle smiled understandingly.

When Rachel later recollected their conversation in the I, she was shocked that she had brought up the subject of her little girl, especially in Isabelle's ethereal company. It had tripped off her tongue almost by accident, as much as she had wanted to keep it securely to herself. It was equally puzzling that she had arranged to meet her new, or old, friend again. She simply had to confront her false story of who she was and get to the bottom of the matter.

She did feel inexplicably close to Isabelle, however. She could be herself around her, perfectly at ease. That was unusual, especially lately, when she hadn't even felt like being with people.

On Saturday, they walked in Walpole Park like two sisters, talking when they felt like it, commenting on the array of flowers and the kids running about wildly, and laughing at the anti-social booming stereo that a man had set up next to him as he slept in the centre of the wide expanse of grass.

They returned to Rachel's flat as it was still early and neither of them had any plans.

More coffee. Isabelle sat in the same place as on the first night she had visited. Rachel had retired to the beanbag on the floor with her back against the pale yellow wall. She looked across at Isabelle's relaxed, assuring expression and sensed that it could wait no longer.

"There's something I've been meaning to ask you."

"Go ahead."

"How do you really know me?"

"What do you mean?" Isabelle seemed unsure whether this was a joke or she had

misunderstood.

"Come on, Isabelle. You know what I mean. Now I don't know what you're playing at, but you know as well as I do that the only friend I ever had called Isabelle was in my head, not real."

Strangely, she felt almost guilty saying it, as though she was deliberately accusing somebody of something they hadn't done.

"Who are you really?" she persisted, unable to stop.

Isabelle laughed with uncertainty. "Rachel...?"

As an empty silence wore on, Rachel began to realise that answers weren't going to come. She's been foolish to expect them.

She thought of her daughter and that mountain she had somehow to climb, or was it a bottomless valley? She didn't have time for fiction.

"You're not who you claim to be," she said with more anger.

"None of us are."

"Oh, don't give me that metaphysical claptrap." Rachel's face flushed.

"Isabelle frowned seriously, cracks that Rachel hadn't noticed before appearing in the skin around her lips.

At length, she spoke. "I'm not sure what you're saying, Rachel, but if you need some time alone, then I'll go." It wasn't a retort, just a suggestion. "I thought we were getting on just fine."

Then Isabelle seemed to become mildly irritated, which was the closest she appeared likely to come to anger. "You know, you can really be cranky at times."

"Perhaps I've got things to be cranky about."

It was useless. She had to order Isabelle to leave or forget about the implausibility of their friendship.

"There's something I've been meaning to ask you as well." Isabelle was as calm as ever again, smiling slightly.

"What?"

What is your daughter's name?"

"Sophie."

It seemed that Isabelle wanted to ask something else but felt restrained by politeness.

"She's five and she lives with her father," Rachel said for her.

"Were you married?"

"Yes," Rachel sighed. "Once. A long time ago."

It had been the last thing she'd wanted to talk about but now she felt a great levity at letting out the stale emotion and despair.

"He found someone more appealing though," she explained without particular bitterness. It seemed like it had been someone else who had lived that life.

"What a fool."

Rachel smiled, grateful but unbelieving. Isabelle, meanwhile, was gazing at the photo on the mantelpiece.

"Do you see her much?" Isabelle's eyes were sympathetic, a little sad.

"No. I don't see her." She looked at the cup in her hands without seeing it. "I wasn't

allowed."

"What?"

"I was drinking."

"But all the same..."

"I still don't see her."

"Why not? Does he prevent you? You can get a court order."

Rachel smiled wryly. "No, it's not that. He doesn't stop me. I stop myself."

"Why? She needs to see you."

"Don't tell me what she needs. And anyway, I wouldn't want her to see me. Let her have grand illusions. That's better than to find out what a hopeless loss I am."

"What are you talking about? That's not true."

"Oh, it is. I've been a bad mother. Too much time has gone by."

"No. You can start again any time."

"I haven't got the heart."

The air seemed to tremble with emotion.

At length, Isabelle spoke again, quietly but with feeling. "Don't you think you owe it to her to give it another try?"

Rachel sat still, rocks in her heart. "Yes. Yes, I do. But I can't. I just can't."

She couldn't bring herself to tell even Isabelle that her impossible dream was to live with Sophie again one day. When she felt brave enough to look up at her friend again, she saw that her eyes were glassy with tears, tears that Rachel had used up a long time ago.

Isabelle insisted on seeing old photos of Sophie. Rachel let herself be persuaded and together they examined the ghosts captured by the camera – effortlessly grinning girl and friends and mum and dad in a utopian past.

By the time Isabelle had to go it was late. They had talked so much that Rachel had just about given up on proving that she couldn't exist.

"I'd better run for that train."

"You know, it's late, Isabelle. You shouldn't catch trains at this time of night."

"You're probably right but I've got to."

"I've got a spare bed in the breakfast room. You can sleep there if you want to."

Isabelle hesitated, clearly preferring this option to struggling back on lonely night trains. "Are you sure?"

"Yes. It's there. You might as well use it. It was Sophie's." Rachel hated the way that every night her daughter's bed lay empty but for memories.

So Isabelle stayed.

During the night, things took on another colour. Rachel came awake in her over-spacious double bed to find a shape hovering above her. The dim orange light from the street outside reflecting off the knife in the figure's hands.

She gasped.

Those eyes, radiant and warm by day, like the sunny rock pools by the sea where they had hunted crabs together, the same eyes had turned into maniacal discs. Her teeth were bared like an animal.

"Mummy," she said.

"Isabelle? Sophie?"

It was a relief when Rachel woke up, still checking the darkness of the big room. She forced herself to get out of bed and creep into the kitchen, to check that her guest was asleep.

She was.

In the morning, Rachel managed to put the disconcerting dream out of her mind as they had breakfast and joked once more.

One night turned into another and before Rachel had had time to think it through properly, Isabelle stayed the whole week. She made Sophie's room her own, and in the evening they went out or chatted together.

If Rachel was tempted to think that she was still imagining her friend's presence, she was comforted that the old Polish couple next door remarked on what a pleasant woman Isabelle was and what a nice smile she had.

When her friend was getting ready to go out, Rachel enjoyed watching her, elegant and professional in a suit or a dress. She began to get quite used to that smile; it had the same effect as opening the morning curtains to sunlight and a perfect blue sky. The flashing eyes and smooth, sandy hair became a part of the flat for a week. She could leave behind thoughts of her own gloomy and disordered life by following Isabelle's movements. It was a joy to see someone so calmly sure of what they were doing.

A splinter of dismay lingered, how"ver,'for Rachel knew that things couldn't last.

The seventh night was Isabelle's last night in Sophie's room. Rachel finished work early on Fridays and sat at home, as before her friend had ever appeared. After tonight, Isabelle would disappear into memory, occasionally phoning to chat perhaps, meeting rarely. It was better not to grow fond of people. Then you wouldn't be hurt when you lost them.

She knew that in the same position, Isabelle would look on the bright side, eagerly anticipating their next meeting. But she wasn't Isabelle, and it all seemed like a waste of time, and worse still, a fantasy. She wished that she was Isabelle, and that in turn made her jealous.

She poured a generous, soothing whisky, but it didn't do its job. She began to feel angry with Isabelle, not for leaving, but for making a mockery of her life by waltzing in from Rachel's imagination and making them hit it off like true friends.

Somewhere along the line of increasingly drunken remonstrances, Rachel 85ealized that Isabelle had taken her mind off her missing daughter, her regrets about the past, and she hated her for this too.

But the flowing alcohol was familiar. She could wrap herself in its protection and feel at home with her shattered hopes, luxuriate in defeatism.

When Isabelle came home late, Rachel had gone to bed early, knocked out by alcohol.

In the morning, she woke up late with a throbbing head and dragged herself from bed.

Isabelle wasn't in her room and Rachel was wondering if she hadn't come home or had already left when she saw the note on the kitchen table.

> Dear Rachel,
> I had to get such an early train and didn't want to wake you. I can't bear goodbyes.
> Can you?
> I hope you see Sophie soon. I'm sure that's

what you want…
…and what she wants.
Give her my love. Just like old times.
We've had a lot of fun. Just like old times.
Love,
Isabelle.

The handwriting was elaborate and natural, but it sounded painfully final and added to the misery of the morning-after. She hadn't even remembered to leave a phone number, but she could get in touch with Rachel easily enough.

When she hadn't heard anything from Isabelle for a week, she tried calling the university where she worked.

Nobody had heard of her, not in the philosophy department, not in any department.

After several attempts, Rachel asked herself if she had somehow got the name of the university confused, but of course she hadn't. Isabelle had even told her all about Durham.

Her confusion was discomfortingly familiar; she had felt the same when Isabelle had first stood outside her door.

There was nothing that she could do but hope that Isabelle would contact her. But her intuition told her not to expect it to happen. All she had were fond memories of the week they had spent together, and of course the memories of their phantasmal time together as small children. And guilt about her unreasonable anger on Isabelle's last night.

Such memories weren't just a fading shadow to cling to. Isabelle, whoever she was, had captured Rachel's affection with her uncomplicated friendliness. She had understood Rachel. With her, she had felt innocent again – like a five-year old – and there had been hope. And Isabelle's eyes and smile were clearly imprinted on her mind.

Six months later, Rachel walked on the beach in Hill Head as she had done so many years ago, at a time when life had been easy.

She gazed at the sky which was thick blue except for three small clouds and a red kite shaking and dancing in the wind. Despite the sun, the sea looked cold and mysterious but a father kicked a football with his son near its edge and a couple passed by with a big, dopey dog on the end of a long piece of rope, padding contentedly along on the sand.

"Mummy, can I have a dog just like that one?" Sophie said as she ran with her kite towards Rachel.

Eyes sparkling, Rachel beamed at her daughter and crouched down with open arms to embrace her playfully. "Maybe one day."

Sophie slipped free and raced her kite away again, the dog temporarily forgotten as she chased a pair of screeching seagulls.

Finding the Plot

Six o' clock: Train

The Toyoko Line, Tokyo to Yokohama

High above the streets, the train pulls out of the giant station. As we cross a bridge up here, I stand awkwardly wedged between the bodies of office workers going home and look through the glass of the door. Yellow lights flicker on and off amidst blue neon lines and red neon signs.

Greens, yellows, whites appear. Massive, anonymous blocks tower over everything, while other tinier ones invite people inside. The cars take centre stage, cruising up and down the main street tyres fizzing on the wet roads. I stare out at the throngs of people. Their umbrellas are held over them like masks, hiding their faces.

I survey the gleaming ads in the train, displayed at every eye-catching angle. A semi-pornographic girl sits coyly, trying to persuade me to buy her magazine. An art museum entices me with slim-waisted, large-breasted Egyptian beauty. Wedding plans, schools and universities all want me and can help me. I stare fixedly at the shiny silver door in resistance, but my eyes are soon drawn back when I forget what I was avoiding. I try looking out of the window again, but the houses stream past too fast, and the darkening sky is a whizzing grey-black blur.

I scan the other passengers, but their faces are all set in perfect horizontal lines. Only their eyes betraying a little disillusion. They never meet my gaze.

At a large station we are told by an announcement that we can change to an express train that will carry us faster, bypassing the smaller stations. As I'm already standing, I get out to change trains. We make long queues outside the doors of the new train, and I watch hordes of passengers pour out with the stench of stale, claustrophobic air. A piercing electronic bell warns us to avoid the closing doors. It sounds before we've even begun to get on, and people hurry anxiously.

Now it's even more crowded. I recoil from the unknown slabs of flesh everywhere but can't escape the fat hands and bony faces pressed up against me. A woman's charmless voice recounts a story to her boyfriend. Someone bumps into me from behind, knocking my legs with something sharp sticking out of a bag, and doesn't apologise. I think I catch a man staring at me with a mean, cruel face. Helplessly, a brutal image erupts in my mind: I picture myself driving a big axe into his head with satisfaction – something I know I'd never do. Raskolnikov comes to mind.

Finally we arrive and spill and tumble out of the train and down the stairs, stepping on each other's heels and barging one another's shoulders. One more short journey will take me home, but I'm so exhausted from the last one that I decide to have a coffee before I press on. I look in the coffee shop right next to the station, only to see that it's completely full. Maybe I'll just get on the next tarin. It's only a fifteen-minute journey anyway.

Whilst I was caught between coffee shop and train, I've just missed one and I stand back on the freezing platform impatiently ruing lost time, as if my happiness depends upon punctually keeping a series of pressing engagements that I don't have.

My mind turns over the little progress I've made. A hundred things to say, jam-packed in my head, but no trace of a story.

I feel like my noble intentions are beginning to desert me. I feel tired and dejected. All the timing in my life is slightly but irrevocably wrong, I think. Who am I to have dreams and be romantic? Just another common fool, who for a moment felt he had something, to say, could do something. At times like this, I only want to lie peacefully in my bed for whole days, warm and ignorant. I can flee from the world and, more importantly, from myself. At times like this, trapped in self-pity, I could lie in a coffin like that steel one near the temple for the rest of time and I'd be peaceful.

…Well, be careful what you wish for, I tell myself. In the midst of a dark, snowy day as it turns to night, it can be hard to remember that the sun is always there somewhere. The snow makes the dirty city look so pretty, like a tiny toy town. But it has made me lose hope inside.

I've been searching for a story. In vain. When you look so hard for something and can't find it, you start to wonder if it's really there at all. You start to doubt your own ability; you doubt your own dreams.

I feel like I'm getting further and further away from what I'm looking for.

But I'm not averse to pursuing a hopeless cause to the grave. I'll flog a dead horse. Discouraged I may be, but I haven't completely lost sight of my starting intentions. And when I can't find something that's important to me, I tend to keep looking. If I really want something – and that's the crucial factor – then it takes a lot for it to elude me.

Maybe that's why I'm still here, still searching.

My six o' clock ruminations are brought to an abrupt halt by a wholly unpredictable encounter. As if chance has been reading my lonely mind, Emma is hovering beside me.

"You look worried," she says and giggles. A smile illuminates my face. The coincidental meeting chases dark thoughts away. It sends packing the unreadable faces of strangers.

Now for real stories. Real people, not unknown ghosts.

Molly

It was a steady job. She'd arrived at nine for the past seven years and not complained once. The machines needed supervision – though sometimes Molly felt *she* was the robot. And there was Suzanna, starting school now.

Why did Molly suddenly question everything? Could you blame it on Autumn – here again?

In the plastic white cafe, she drank three cups of coffee – slowly – just thinking… "I don't have to do this."

Her life flashed before her.

Things could be different.

Then she paid her bill, and walked briskly over the road to work, apologising for her lateness.

Finding the Plot

Seven o' clock: Real People

Yokohama City

"I'm meeting the others in Souled Out,*" Emma tells me. I don't know who others are but together we set off, my mind brimming with the potential, at last, for a story.*

We catch up on the short walk there, but for some reason prefer silence in the tiny, bright yellow glare of the elevator. Looking like she knows exactly what she'll find inside, she pushes open the nondescript black door – they don't broadcast their whereabouts here. It's like a secret society. I follow her into the bar, a gloomy, smoke-ridden space on the fifth floor of a decrepit-looking building. I hope I'll find something inside, too – a spark of inspiration amongst the shadowed faces.

The others are assembled at a long, black table in the centre of the room heads bobbing up and down in cheerful conversation. They look up as Emma approaches and their smiles grow wider. I join the table and glance over at the waiter, who doubles up as the barman, lingering in the background, waiting to make his move. I look around at the half-lit faces at other tables, gathered here to drown disappointments or celebrate half-successes.

The alcohol is already beginning to flow, undulating conversations lapping over one another. And what better place to find my story? I study the characters at the table, people I know but haven't seen for a long while, scrutinizing their faces for something – anything that might hint at a story plot. The low lighting giving me perfect camouflage to study them, allowing me to slip into the background and observe these real people.

Emma doesn't say much. I watch her, immediately teasing Nicki about something that I can't catch, laughing good-naturedly as she gets ribbed back. Nicki takes a slug from a bottle of golden liquid. Emma orders a large beer from the waiter, a thin man with a tired smile, who has floated up to us, and says to me,

"Same for you, Toki?"

"Thank you. I'm writing at the moment, though, so I'm going to pass." I speak to the waiter: "A mineral water, if you have one."

She giggles conspiratorially. "The man with the plans," she says.

I laugh. "Not exactly. I'm just a little engrossed with it at the moment." I smile. "Gotta keep a clear head."

Daisuke, Nicki's boyfriend, joins in. "Emma, you must have plans too, right?"

She giggles shyly. "What? Me? Plans? I don't make plans."

"Oh, fair enough," he says.

"Tokiya makes plans." she says, pointing at me to divert the attention away from herself. "He's got it all sorted out. Ask him! He's the one who knows what he's doing."

"Hardly," I reply.

I feel her thigh touch against mine, involuntarily, under the table. She feels warm and reassuring. I take a look sideways at her, remembering how pretty she is. Her smile is like the warm sun peeping through the clouds in a winter sky. She's quiet but fun. Unassuming but important. She's that person who makes sure that people get leaving presents, birthday cards, wedding gifts.

"Anyway, a good tactic," I add with mock irritation. "Pass the buck. After all, Tokiya almost got married."

There's an unhealthy pause following this comment, and I realise that it's not something that other people feel comfortable with. They don't know what to say. They look at each other as though they know something that I don't, as though reminded of something they preferred to forget.

Only Daisuke, ever the innocent one, doesn't seem in on the secret.

"What went wrong?" he says.

"Timing," I say. "I think it was timing."

"How do you mean?"

I don't have to answer as Bill is interrogating Emma.

"Why don't you ever make plans, Emma? You must make some, come on."

She puffs nervously at her cigarette.

"Look, I just don't know," she laughs, and shakes her head self-consciously, literally trying to shoo the conversation away to someone else with her hands. "Ask someone else."

I watch her quietly refuse the meat-topped pizza that arrives, and I help the vegetarian one down the table towards her.

"I don't save money either," she says.

"I can imagine Emma in twenty years," Nicki is saying. "You'll be the kind of mother who can share a beer with your teenage sons."

"Oh my God. I've got a long way to go first. I think I need to find a man first."

"And you'll shout at them but still be friends with them."

Emma groans.

"I think we're talking about the distant future here," she says.

Finding a partner can't be far off with her exotic Chinese looks and appealing hesitation.

I listen as the conversations overlap, a mix of work complaints, weekend plans (except for Emma), and thinly veiled flirtations. Nothing particularly stands out. I feel the old, creeping dread – maybe there is nothing here after all.

Nicki is relating a pointless new rule in the office when Emma turns to me and says, her voice softer, "Bought any good CDs recently?"

Long ago, when she'd first arrived in the country, I'd given her a tour of central Yokohama, showing her cheap places to get a good meal and the best second-hand music shops.

"Yeah, I bought one the other day actually. Tears For Fears." I wait for her verdict, as if I wrote the music myself.

She giggles, a tinkling sound incongruent with the heavy room. "That's a bit old, isn't it?"

"That's just good music, plain and simple. Timeless."

"You've always been an old soul, Toki."

Emma's gentle way can melt your heart, but at the same time I don't want to be an old soul. I want to be a writer with a story to tell. I need purpose and direction. Perhaps she's right about me being a maker of plans.

Bill has caught something of our conversation and begins a rendition of Change, singing not only the words but the parts of the musical instruments too. Daisuke laughs nervously at his antics.

I survey the table. These are friends, or people who were once friends, and yet I feel like I'm watching them from behind a glass pane, separate somehow.

Scott, on my right, is drinking a bottle of Corona with a slice of lime wedged in the neck. He elbows me playfully and says,

"What do you think, mate? You've always got a perspective on things."

He grins and I think of easygoing Australians basking in the sun. I realise that I haven't kept up with the conversation and quickly fish back through the words still echoing around the table from something that Nicki has said: something about her boss's latest meltdown. She's gesturing wildly, her beer sloshing in its glass. The room feels far away – the clinking glasses and hum of voices like something from another life.

I feel like I've forgotten my lines but no-one seems to notice when I stumble for a suitable reply.

Emma glances at me and leans in.

"You're quiet tonight, Toki. Lost in thought?"

I smile. "Just soaking it all in," I reassure her.

She nods but I spot a flicker of confusion pass across her face like a fleeting shadow.

"I have exactly no artistic talent," Nicki is saying.

"That's not true," Daisuke chimes in.

"It is!" She pokes him in the belly. "You do. You play the guitar."

"I try," he laughs.

"How's your painting coming on, Emma?" Scott asks her.

"I'm doing some."

"More birds and temples?" Bill teases her.

She gives him the finger. "Not so much, actually."

"Go on," he encourages her. "Tell us more."

I can see she would prefer to keep it to herself, let her paintings do their own talking to those who behold them.

"More abstract things, these days," she says, playing with a beer mat, her eyes secretly dancing.

"Abstract!" Scott says. "Very intellectual."

"Hardly."

"Shapes and so on?" Bill asks.

I notice that he looks at her with wider eyes than he has for the rest of them. He teases her but also seems to hang on her words. I suspect that he has a crush on her but something secret. And I don't mind Bill but for some reason I hope that she doesn't end up with him.

"You'll laugh!" she laughs.

"We won't!" they say.

"The most recent things I've done are all in ink: a black square and a white square."

They all laugh, not maliciously but because they know she won't mind and it does sound funny when she says it.

"The black square I get," Scott says. "But how the hell do you paint a white square with ink?"

"Well… that'd be telling," she chides him.

I find myself wondering what would be equivalent to a black and a white square in the world of stories.

"I prefer something more …tangible," Daisuke says.

Emma turns to me. "Didn't you start painting?"

I remember her giving me some pointers one lunchtime, little tips and tricks to set me on my way.

"I tried it once," I say. "But the artistic talent in my family seems to have skipped a generation."

"Hmm. You look as though you should be doing something artistic," Scott tells me.

"The charade is working," I joke.

"That's true," Bill joins in. "Tokiya, you always look as though you're far off somewhere else."

"Do I?"

"Yeah, like you want something, like you're looking for

something. What's going on inside your head?" Bill says.

"Nothing of note," I say. "There are birds inside my head, I think."

"What kind of birds?" Nicki asks, squawking with amusement.

Emma answers for me. "Crows, definitely."

She knows me better than I had expected.

"And what are you looking for?" Scott asks me.

"Huh?"

"Well, Bill thinks you look as if you're searching for something."

"I guess I'm trying to find …the right story."

There's a pause and the bar seems to have gone quiet. Then Nicki, ever quick to fill a silence, convulses with laughter. "You won't find it here, that's for sure!"

"Sorry," Daisuke smiles. "She's always like this after a few beers!"

She strokes his hair.

The table joins in with the laughter and I smile along. At the same time, I feel a weightlessness. Perhaps I'm just tired from my day in the city amongst the zombies. I look down at my hands, and dig a fingernail into my palm, feeling an urge to make sure I'm real, that I'm really here.

"Well, I guess I'll head out," I say after a while.

"Already? You okay?" Emma says.

"Fine. Just a little tired."

They murmur their goodbyes and I pull on my coat, which feels heavy on my shoulders.

As I reach the door, I see Emma mouth the words, "Take care," and there is melancholy look in her black eyes.

Back down in the rickety elevator. Outside, I reacquaint myself with the freezing air, then shiver and tremble towards the station, cursing the absence of even warmer clothes. Something is wrong with the weather. It's unnaturally cold for this time of year, isn't it? Or have I just forgotten that it was exactly the same last year, and the year before? It seems impossible to remember, for some *reason.*

I'm isolated and at a loss once again. I stop in the frozen street. Am I expecting too much? I crave perfect characters for the perfect story. A blue sky to hang above everything. Is there something wrong with me? Still there isn't a story in sight – despite the people, the conversation, the bar.

I smile, though, as Emma's gentle smile comes to my mind and I think of her thigh accidentally brushing up next to mine. That gives me hope and I pick up my pace, passing groups of young people laughing loudly.

The city stretches out around me, vast and indifferent. A woman bumps into me, brushing shoulders, as we cross paths and she apologises. Her face seems blurred to me from the sudden unexpected motion and, for a second, I see Emma's features in her – the shiny, thick black hair, the slightly square jaw, the dancing eyes. But it's not her. It's someone else; maybe it's no-one.

Storyless, despite the real people I've hung out with, I carry on my way through the colourfully-lit night-time streets, still searching. It feels as though I'm not so much looking for something I must find as seeking something I have lost, or that was never even there.

The Upstairs Room

i. The Upstairs Room

The paper was blank. A white square.

I didn't care for its clean veneer but I'd been struggling to portray the bird in my head with the discordant, twisted mood that I wanted. There were crumpled up balls of paper in the corner of the small room.

I laid down my brush and gave up again. Went to bed, where I lay next to Bill, who snored an apocalyptic maelstrom of red wine fumes.

I heard a sound. Somebody whimpering. Or crying.

I woke up more fully.

It was sex. Upstairs, a couple were conjoining in bliss and expressing their ecstasy with soft moans and occasional yelps. My loins began to smoulder.

I touched Bill's back, ran a finger down his spine, put a cold toe against the sole of his foot. I waited to see if the corpse stirred, but it didn't.

The moans and yelps continued for what seemed the longest time. I rued that it never lasted that long in my experiences. But finally they must have had their satisfaction and the sound was no more, replaced by the pregnant silence of the dark.

I fell asleep and dreamt of nothing. It was a good dream.

In the morning, Bill had apparently resuscitated and gone to work. I started later than he did. I fed his birds and made a mental note to tell him that that wasn't my job; they were his birds. I didn't even like having birds in the house.

Two black coffees and I managed to get out of the flat. Instead of going straight out, I put my head around the corner of the stairwell and snuck a look at the impassive front door of the upstairs flat, as though that would reveal something about the secrets of discovering good sex and a loving relationship, or just the faces and personalities of its occupants.

The door was ajar. It was too much to resist. I only hesitated for half a breath before I went up and silently stood in front of the door.

The sensible thing would have been to go straight to work, no nonsense, no nosiness. But I guess I was bored. My page was blank and this was an image to fill it.

Number 13 on the door; what a cliché.

No moans of pleasure; no breakfast sounds; a cold silence.

I assumed that the lovers had gone to work and failed to properly close the door.

The sensible thing would have been to mind my own business, to go back down the stairs, to head out and go to work.

I called out, "Hello?"

I looked inside.

Something was off. It was one of those feelings that you can't immediately put a finger on. Your senses have perceived the details that tell you all is not quite as it should be.

I pushed the door slightly more open and it yielded without objection.

There wasn't anything unpleasant about the empty flat. But it *was* empty. In fact, it was uninhabited. The living room was empty: no furniture, no bookshelves, no curtains, no carpet. I went into the main bedroom. The shape was exactly like our flat downstairs. It was empty, too. No bed on which wonderful lovers copulated for what seemed like an hour or more. Like the living room, there was nothing there.

The kitchen, bathroom and second bedroom were the same. There was nothing squalid or abandoned about the flat; it was simply uninhabited and empty.

…Except for one thing.

The second bedroom, the smaller of the two, had a painting on the wall.

It just about qualified as a painting. It was a black square slightly larger than a laptop screen. I went closer and examined its blackness, checking if the strokes were real. Sure enough, these were brush strokes. Its frame was wooden and painted black. I retreated and cocked my head on one side, letting the black square wash over my consciousness. It was as inscrutable as the empty flat; null and void.

So who had been making love in this flat? Had I dreamt it?

I turned to go, remembering my life and my job.

I hadn't dreamt it; I was sure of that.

My heart skipped a beat as I was about to leave the flat. I saw a woman moving in the bathroom. Then I recovered as I realised I had missed one other thing – a small mirror in the bathroom, which flashed my reflection at me through the open door.

I had the impression that the person reflected wasn't myself. That must have been the strange place getting to me. I shook my head and went to work, leaving the door ajar.

ii. The Manipulators

I spent the day in the office, as usual, as always, a paid player in a funeral dance that led nowhere.

I wasn't sure how it had come to this. I hadn't wanted to go to university, not particularly, but then I had gone to university, majoring in Art History and Vodka Studies. I'd come out with a good degree and a future as a paid monkey in a succession of multi-person, desk-filled coffins that made money for *the Man* and tax for the government, but didn't seem to do much for most of the people working there – with the exception of the Chief Manipulators. (The Chief Manipulators were the advertising execs, a special breed of liar adept in persuading Joe Public to spend his wages on things he didn't need and couldn't afford.)

The boss, Dennis Baller, owner of Baller and Sons, who had no son but this was all about illusion, wasn't it, smoke and mirrors, the art of persuasion (if you can use the sacred word *art* about such lies), had in my last performance review instructed me that I had the potential to become a CM. It seemed that just by osmosis, I had been in the environment for so long that I was beginning to move effortlessly amongst the jargon of information commercials. He liked my no-nonsense attitude, he said. It could be an asset. And my attention to detail. And he liked that at the Christmas parties, I could hold my spirits and keep up with the big boys. I suspected that this last point was the main thing in my favour when it came to questions of promotion.

I couldn't deny that I'd take a promotion to CM. There'd be lots more money. Think of the doors that would open: travel, new equipment, courses I could take, a new apartment. I might leave Bill, I considered. Find a place with my own dedicated studio where I could invite an artistic crowd – intellectual and fun, but not pretentious and greedy – I could leave his menagerie of birds behind, his drinking, his apathy.

The CMs worked long hours but they didn't work harder. There was corporate socialising, travel, all-nighters on next morning deadlines. None of that appealed. I liked to go to bed at the same time every day: 11:55. It was a superstition with me, I suppose, to beat the 12:00 Cinderella hour; it went back to school days and seeming to get spots all over my face if I made it to bed a minute later than midnight.

Did I want to work with that bunch of arrogant, slick cynics anyway? It wouldn't leave me much time to work on my paintings, and I'd be using precious energy on changing my mindset to the lying mode.

Dennis had said, "You're a natural liar, Dinah," and laughed his flame-thrower of a laugh.

"Don't take that the wrong way," he added. "It's a compliment. What I mean to say is that you keep things to yourself. You're sort of…" He searched his mind for the right word. "You're inaccessible. Inscrutable. No-one really knows what you're thinking."

He shot me a wicked glance.

"Thank you?" I asked.

Of course it was second nature for a man like Dennis Baller to feel a need to manipulate and persuade me of something. That was his raison d'etre, the same as I had to think about representing ideas in paint.

And maybe we weren't so different in the end. I wanted to manipulate my currently non-existent viewers into a reaction, a mental or visceral response to what I had created. The main difference was that my work was unseen, and unrewarded, whereas Baller drove a Maserati, wore expensive suits and took holidays in the Bahamas.

iii. The Lasting Impression

In the little office kitchen, as I cleaned the coffee pot in the sink, I wasn't thinking about advertising campaigns or promotions. Absent-mindedly, I washed away the stains in the white mug. I set it on the sideboard to drain. Then I took out the plunger of the cafetiere. I found myself staring into the grouts of coffee like a fortune teller reading tea leaves, looking for hidden meaning. They were packed into a solid hive of soft, sweet grouts, a black wall... I recalled the one item in the flat upstairs, a painting, a simple square of black. All other thought was far from my mind. The past and future, even the present, had ceased to be.

I knew that I would return to the upstairs flat and drink in that strange black square again, as though it had a message to give me, a scripture to decode.

I thought of the luxurious sounds of ecstasy. They mingled in my consciousness with little kitchen I stood in now, the city traffic down below, the tap running into the steel sink, the din of clacking keyboards in the open plan office next door. The sounds of furious typing was a war-cry of drums and returned me to my consciousness. Nearby, there was the urgent beeping of a reversing lorry.

Dennis himself came into the kitchen and I straightened.

"*Someone's in the kitchen with Dinah...*" he began singing with bonhomie. "You all right, my darling? You look as though you've seen a ghost."

He wasn't far off the truth, I considered. Who the hell had been copulating in an abandoned flat, with no bed linen, no bed, no furniture. Okay, it was good to be primal and do it on the floor sometimes, but it seemed unlikely that anyone had been there at all. But I'd heard the sounds. ...Unless somehow they were sounds from a different flat that had seemed to come from directly above.

I went back to my work but I was distracted all afternoon.

I left at 5 on the dot, grabbing my hat and coat and fleeing the building as fast as I could.

Normally, I walked around for a few minutes in between changes of train line, and often went to a little art shop hidden away in a back street, selling works by hidden away painters who no-one had ever heard of. But today, I jumped on the second train without delay and soon I was walking quickly up my street, unlocking the side door that led to our flat.

I passed my own front door and carried on up to the abandoned flat. I listened outside its entrance for signs that I had imagined the whole visit last night – that in fact there was life unfolding in a perfectly normal way inside – but all was still.

Gingerly, I pushed the front door and it yielded without even a squeak.

The empty flat had the familiarity of a second visit now. Quickly I took in the echoey space, the cold stillness. I walked to the small bedroom.

Still there. Nothing had changed.

In a white room devoid of furniture and furnishings, a square of blackness on the wall. I searched its inscrutable strokes. As I looked, the strokes of paint seemed to sway, almost imperceptibly, and morph into each other, but that was a trick of the eyes, for sure. I went closer.

My body registered a kind of static voltage, like drinking a whole cafetiere of coffee all at once. There was a strange blend of both fear and lust coursing through my veins, as though I stood on the threshold of a doorway to a mysterious new place – which, although I didn't know it then, was exactly what I was doing.

After ten or fifteen minutes, I wrenched myself away and went downstairs and into the screeching, twittering din of my own flat.

iv. The Love

Bill was home when I got back. He usually left before me and arrived home after me, so it was a surprise.

"Hello," he managed. "I'm going to do some writing."

"Okay."

He sloped off into the study, carrying a tumbler of whisky and a glass. He seemed to think he was Hemingway or Kerouac, but I'd never seen him produce more than a banal short story about hedonistic alcoholics and partygoers. Once, in what seemed another lifetime, I'd taken an interest and supported him, encouraging him to tell me about his ideas and his progress. He'd always been reticent and over time, his words retreated further and further into the recesses of his brain – until we argued and then it flooded out in torrents of anger.

Perhaps I should have been smart enough to spot red flags, but we had been very young. I had taken his lack of interest in my painting as acceptance and non-judgment; I had imagined that it was tacit support.

I sensed that he blamed me for keeping him from a wild life as a journalistic vagabond. He'd told me as much in the heat of disagreements. It wasn't true. I hadn't stopped him from doing anything, either physically or psychologically. As far as I could see, it was an excuse for his apathy. Then again, if only I could have found some way of reaching behind his walls. I did blame myself for not being able to find the magic word or gesture to unlock his defences.

Fate had conspired to throw us together at the after-work gatherings to let off steam in our previous jobs. I'd been drawn to his shy smile and nervousness, wanting to find out more. I'd read into his love of wild animals that he was a kind and caring soul. And of course he was a fellow artist, mentioning his commitment to writing in the early morning.

There had been a time when he had been happy to move into our flat in the suburbs – unless he'd been hiding it very well indeed. We'd made love – at least, we'd had sex; looking back, I don't think we could call it *making love*. We had talked about art and literature, watched French films together at the British Film Institute. He even started writing a book about French cinema and I encouraged him, making him cups of coffee and sandwiches. He was a much better non-fiction writer than crafter of stories, in my opinion, but I only offered this insight tentatively. Maybe I should have been more forthright.

But all of that too had died a death. Neither of us would have been able to pin-point the moment when the relationship was no longer working, but it had been long ago, years ago, and it was impossible to imagine a return from that moment. One argument too many? One causally thrown insult that left a serious wound? He'd said I was shit in bed. That didn't help our sex life. When someone says you're no good at something, you don't feel like rewarding them for their honesty, even it was true. ...And wasn't he complicit in that, anyway?

I sat on the sofa, amongst his cages of birds, and drank a cup of tea on my own. But my artistic visions, which he had also derided on more than one occasion – "Do you actually think your paintings are good?" – filled my head, and I thought of the flat upstairs, and I considered whether I could somehow do it ghostly justice in ink paint. Could I capture the weirdness of the night before with the gentle endeavour of my sweeping paint brush?

I thought about switching on the TV, sitting in the corner, collecting a dusty sheen. My thoughts were interrupted by occasional, startling bird noises. In his space next door, divorced from me, I could hear the clatter of the keys as Bill spoke to the blank page. The noise always escalated to rattling, then clanking and finally crashing, the more he drank. But nothing ever seemed to emanate the form of readable words. And the next sound I would hear from Bill would be his snores, as I crept into bed after him.

This night would depart from the norm.

Bill was snoring as usual. If we'd lived in a larger place, I would've gone to sleep somewhere else, but the only option was currently the sofa in his zoo, which was definitely not an option. Rain was pattering on the window panes. The street outside was quiet apart from an occasional, distant siren.

I began to drift into a slumber, the shape of poignant dreams crowding in on my consciousness, when a cry lifted me straight back to wakefulness.

I knew immediately what it was. My eyes were wide open, searching the darkness for something that wasn't there. My whole being was collected in my ears, straining to hear something.

Again it came, a soft, blissful moaning of pleasure from a woman. Muffled grunts from a man. Then cries of soft pleasure overlapping each other like waves cavorting on a sun-strewn seashore, tickling at the shingle, swishing upon the sand, specks of diamond light flickering and dancing on the mirror of the ocean surface.

I lay there for a short while. Then I knew what I had to do.

If I wasn't going to be plagued by question marks about my own sanity, I had to go and see. Before I had the inclination to hesitate, I grabbed a large pullover from the cupboard, and my mobile phone from the bedside table for a flashlight.

The moans were louder than yesterday; the pleasure sounded more intense, almost painful.

I went up the stairs, my head filling with the crashing of blood and adrenalin. I took the stairs two at a time.

I paused only for a brief second outside the door of the upstairs flat. It was open, so I could almost pretend that I wasn't intruding.

Perhaps because I didn't really believe what I was hearing, I just went in. If there were really people fornicating in the abandoned flat above ours and I arrived to disturb them, I ought to be scared of their reaction. But it didn't cross my mind.

Into the flat I marched, as I had approximately seventeen hours earlier.

I couldn't yet see them but could hear that the woman was reaching orgasm, that I knew for sure.

The sound of gentle laughing from her partner.

…A shared joke.

She sighed.

It was coming from the room with the picture. They were coming in the room with the picture. The door was open. I shone my mobile flashlight into the darkness and sensuality.

v. The Darkness

Everything I was picturing from the noises evaporated at the same time as the sounds disappeared, sucked into a black hole in the room. Swallowed up by a void, they cried out no more.

I stood there, convinced that I was a raving lunatic; there was something wrong with the wiring in my brain.

What ghosts were these? I hadn't conjured up those sounds in my head. Gaping into the black space of the room, I was as sure of that fact as when I had heard them with my own ears, just moments ago.

There was a zen paradox that asked whether a tree falling in an empty forest, with no-one there to perceive it, still made a sound. This was the opposite. There was no tree, and yet I had heard it fall. I could hear its echoes in my brain.

I stood in the darkness, coming to terms with an inexplicable situation. I felt like I was in a strange film or a book. The silence rang in my ears.

Had I imagined those sounds? I knew that I hadn't; I thought that I hadn't.

But this couldn't go on, that was for sure.

I walked around the flat, going from room to room with my flashlight. Nothing stirred, apart from my own reflection in the bathroom mirror, peering back at me, wondering who I was.

Finally, I went back to the small bedroom, walked up to the black square on the wall, and made up my mind. I reached out two hands, and took it carefully down from its picture hook.

I turned and left the room, walked out of the flat, back down the stairs, into my own flat, closed and locked the front door, and went back into the bedroom. I'd decide the next day what to do with the picture. For the time being, I slid it face down underneath my side of the bed.

I went straight to sleep, pausing only for a second to wonder why I had stolen a picture from another flat. Then again, what I had done was no more peculiar than hearing sounds that didn't exist.

As I drifted off, there were no voices or cries in the dark. At last, my body felt completely at ease, wholly relaxed.

I did dream strange things. And so did Bill, as it turned out.

It would be easy to take a mystical line of argument: the stolen picture underneath the bed was sending waves of weirdness into our sleeping consciousness. That would be the kind of thing to happen on television.

Whatever the cause, whether it was the steak that we'd eaten, a noise from the street outside, or just a random coincidence, we both dreamt of the woman in the forest.

vi. The Dreams

He was making coffee when I came into the kitchen. The pod coffee maker was gurgling and spewing out a thick brew.

"Good morning", I said.

He turned and I saw he couldn't have slept as well as I did. The habitual bags under his eyes were more cavernous than usual. His face looked almost yellow, like a freshly dug up corpse.

"Morning," he croaked.

I cocked my head on one side. "You okay?"

He scratched his head and ruffled his morning mess of hair.

"Bizarre dreams," he frowned. "Maybe it's the story I'm working on. Or I might be coming down with something."

"Oh?"

We didn't tell each other our dreams, hadn't for years now. It wasn't a cruel or callous indifference; we had just outgrown that level of interest in each other. And he had tended not to remember his dreams, unlike me. So I was surprised that he was telling me about whatever visions the night had conjured up for his sleeping mind.

"A woman in a clearing amongst some trees. She was wearing a mask. It was really eerie."

I stared at him.

"Really strange," he repeated. He saw me looking at him oddly. "What's wrong?"

My throat was dry. I felt a shiver caress my spine.

"I dreamt that, too."

I must have said it too quietly.

"What, sorry?"

"I dreamt the same thing," I said more loudly.

He gave me a puzzled look.

"What do you mean?"

"A woman in a forest. Feeding pieces of paper into…"

"…a fire," he said, as though we were soulmates finishing each other's sentences, not estranged housemates who had wound up in each other's way.

"Yes," I said gravely.

We looked at each other in silence.

He took his coffee cup from the coffee maker. He seemed to have to concentrate hard on what he was doing, as though he had never held a cup before.

"Well this is weird," he said, finally.

"Very."

"How can it be?"

My mind turned to the painting under the bed but, even then, I didn't really give the idea that it might have caused these dreams any credibility.

"I don't know," I said.

"Maybe it's something we saw on TV."

"We didn't watch TV," I reminded him.

"Or on Facebook, or Twitter… I don't know."

"I don't do social media."

He mumbled, "Must be an explanation."

He was right but I couldn't think of one.

"It was unsettling," he said. "Made me feel really awful when I woke up. Did you feel the same?"

"Not really."

More likely, I considered, he felt awful because he'd had one too many whiskeys while he slaved over a short story that would never see the light of day.

He grunted. "Must be something subliminal that caused it. I wonder if it's ever happened before to us, without us knowing."

"I doubt it," I said.

Again, for some reason, I found myself thinking of the painting lying under the bed like stolen goods. Well, it was stolen goods.

"I need to get ready for work," he said, carrying his coffee out of the kitchen.

That was the most we had conversed for quite some time, all because of the odd dream that we'd had both had.

The working day took over. No-one I spoke to had had any strange dreams. They certainly hadn't seen, in their sleeping mind's eye, a ghostly woman in a long, white dress, solemnly feeding pieces of paper into a fire, in a clearing in the trees.

vii. The Awakening

It was unremarkable Friday but the evening held surprises in store.

Bill was home before me. He was reading a book in the living room. Something was cooking on the stove in the kitchen. We had once cooked for each other but, somewhere along the line, he'd derided a meal that I made one time to many and now we only catered for ourselves.

"You all right?" I said, putting my head around the living room door.

He looked up from the book. "There's actually enough for you, if you're hungry."

"Oh!" I couldn't help my surprise. "Thank you."

He mumbled and went back to reading.

I was hungry, but once I had taken off my coat, I busied myself with hanging the black square in my little painting room. It was a box room but the painting wasn't large. Again I felt as if I was handling stolen property and if anyone should come to our flat enquiring about a missing picture, I'd simply return it and face whatever consequences there might be. Perhaps I'd make up some lie about it being left outside my door, I mused.

Bill must have passed by as I was putting it in place on a hook above my painting table.

For someone who had habitually taken so little interest, almost religiously so, it was unnerving to turn and see him watching me closely. But once I'd hung the picture, I realised he wasn't looking at me at all, but the painting.

In the old days, I would've said to him, "Do you like it?" or "What do you think it means?" But I no longer considered his opinion.

He went on staring at it, even venturing a couple of steps into the room, which was sacrilege; he was transgressing an unwritten rule. The room was so small, too, that we were standing awkwardly on the edge of each other's boundaries.

As he gazed into the space between the four frames, his eyes were far away, as though he was awake but dreaming. I had things to do and moved past him, out of the room. Ten minutes later, going to the kitchen, I noticed he was still there, rooted to the spot, looking at the picture, saying nothing as I pointedly cleared my throat and came back into the room.

When I went to bed, I felt him once again staring, this time at me, as I put on my pyjamas. I put it out of my mind and got into bed, grateful that we had bought a king-size that afforded me lots of space all to myself.

As I went to sleep, images from the day collected in my consciousness. I drifted into the night time abyss and was soon dreaming, a woman in white standing over a fire, amongst the trees. I wanted to know what she was dropping into the flames. What was on those pieces of paper? Letters? Photographs? Memories?

Later on, another dream: it wasn't other people's sounds of pleasure that I heard, but my own. In the shadows of the night, my lover caressed my hair, kissed my cheek, nibbled the space between my neck and shoulder. A finger beneath the sheets drew an electric line from my thigh to my hip, and then then... My mind was inside-out. The place where he ended and I began blurred. Time melted. Ripples of pleasure grew… Waves of ecstasy crashed…

By morning, the loving dream had long since crumbled away.

Bill was awake, reading his book again, but in bed this time. It was unprecedented. It was Saturday, but I couldn't recall the last time he hadn't already been up and long gone, or else still sleeping in the foggy throes of a hangover, by the time I was awake. It occurred to me that he hadn't had anything to drink the night before.

He looked at me and said, "Hey."

I saw the same look in his eyes as when he'd gazed at the picture. Who was this person?

Surreptitiously, I eased the duvet up to cover my shoulders.

"Hi," I said cautiously from my cocoon.

Did he know what I had been dreaming, I wondered. And close on the heels of that thought: Had he also had a dream like that?

He smiled and carried on reading. Something had possessed him, I thought. I wondered if he was up to something. Maybe he was having an affair.

"Er, I was wondering…" he said.

Here we go, I thought. I knew that something wasn't right.

"Shall we go and get a coffee in that new place around the corner?" He was speaking to his book, without looking up, and for a moment wondered if he was talking to me.

"Coffee?" I said.

"Yeah. Don't have to – if you'd rather not," he added quickly.

I propped myself up with a pillow.

"New place? Is there a new place?"

"Yes. I think it's called the *Missing Bean*, or something."

I felt I was at a crossroads. I didn't want to take a wrong step and end up in a place I didn't want to be. But it was just a coffee.

"You can paint afterwards," he said. "And I'll do some writing."

We went for a coffee. He was talkative in the café. We were like strangers. That wasn't a bad thing.

When we left the café, it had started raining, thick lines of water coming down at angles and lashing the street and the pavement. He had an umbrella – where had that sprung from? – and he held it over both of us, keeping us a little bit dry.

And later, after sat for a while beneath the inscrutable black canvas, working on an inky crow on a bough, I made two toasted sandwiches with mozzarella, tomato and basil leaves, one for me and one for Bill. I took it to him in the study and he turned and smiled. I only saw the screen behind him for a moment, as he took the plate from me, but I felt that the words there were ordered and clear.

What I was thinking? Surely I was seeing things that weren't there again – or perhaps seeing what I wanted to see. I went and ate my toastie, scrolling through the news on my phone and planning which exhibitions to visit.

I was washing up when I heard him come into the kitchen.

He put his plate on the side of the sink.

"Thank you. That was really nice."

"You're welcome," I said to the stranger.

We shared a smile. I met his gaze. I'd forgotten how grey his eyes were.

I turned back to the chore but an instant later felt him wrapping his arms around my waist from behind.

Another crossroads. I could bat him away. I could shout at him, ask him what the hell he was doing. I could ignore him.

I remembered the dream, the ghostly lovers upstairs, the strange painting whose strokes seemed to swirl and change as you beheld them.

I turned to face him and we kissed. He looked at me with affection – normal, honest affection. It came back to me how I had once found him cool and attractive. We held hands, the first time in an age.

Then we were in the bedroom.

viii. The Upstairs Room

Shortly after, people moved into the flat upstairs.

There were distant noises from above in the night time, sometimes, but they didn't keep me awake. We had noises of our own.

Molly and Pierre were artists, as it happened, and it didn't take long to become friendly with them. She had quit her job several years ago to devote herself to her painting and had had some measure of success in small galleries outside London. He was a house painter and sculpted in his free time. We all had a lot to talk about and they were open and easygoing.

Shortly after moving in, they held a housewarming party and Bill and I went up to make an appearance. It was strange being back there. I kept my secret close to my heart but as I stepped across the threshold, I felt a bit like a voyeur, or a ghost refrequenting an earlier scene.

The flat looked nothing like before, though. They had made it into something vibrant and arty, Moroccan lanterns, jewelled mirrors and wall tapestries in the hallway, tiles with intricate, geometric patterns in the kitchen, cushions and thick rugs in the living room. It was unrecognisable. There was soft lighting. There was laughter. There were people. It felt like I'd been there in a different life. Things had changed so much since then.

"I love what you've done with it," I said, accepting a glass of wine.

Bill shook his head and declined. "I'll just have a sparkling water, if you've got one," he said. "I'm on a health drive and all that."

"Did you ever see it before we moved in?" Molly asked.

"No," I said quickly.

"I'll give you a guided tour, if you like," she smiled. She looked at me with unguarded, dark eyes.

"Sure," I said.

I followed her around the small flat, passing brightly painted pots and pictures of white buildings on hillsides. She pointed out a photograph, explained the significance of a painting, here and there.

She opened the door to the bedroom. I half-expected to see it as it had been – uninhabited and bare.

Of course, it was furnished with the same careful attention, soft reds and purples. There was a dresser with a hairbrush, stray blonde locks in its teeth, and a lipstick next to it. An ochre candle stood on a bedside table.

On the wall opposite the bed hung a painting. It seemed out of keeping with the others in the flat.

At first, I had to look more closely to check that it wasn't an empty frame, but it wasn't. You could make out the strokes of paint when you peered more carefully, white contours swirling this way and that.

A white square.

Finding the Plot

Eight o'clock: City at Night

Yokohama City

The city at night is a different story. It doesn't sleep.

Perhaps it's it reveals its secrets only in the dark. I feel different beneath the silky, black veil above us, as if my true being only comes out at night.

Its intensity is different – intensely playful, no longer obsessed with deadlines. The whole meaning of time changes. Men and women suddenly have all the hours in the world to stop and listen to a jazz band bellowing out its tunes. Up and down and up and down goes the saxophone, as if locked in endless kinetic energy; its player bends and straightens again, bows all the way, leans back again, in perfect synchronicity with his tune – a priest performing holy rites to his god. The song drifts on and on contentedly, a mirror of the small crowd that has gathered to listen.

Then all of a sudden it stops and folk shuffle off on their way again; a few more take their places. I'm at the back, on the fringe (as ever), half on my way and half-watching. The music seems distant and dreamy.

I watch some young lads chuckling, punching and kicking each other as they wait around at a large pillar. The sound of their laughter seems muffled to me as though underwater. They in turn watch two young women who link arm in arm and waltz lopsidedly towards the station. Businessmen in raincoats crowd together and stumble along, propping each other up and smiling. The barriers are down and the alcohol gushes through.

At the station, there is an innocent-eyed girl waiting outside the entrance, still in grown-up work clothes. The serious working day is behind her; ahead lie cafes, bars or restaurants where she will talk and laugh and drink, drink and confide and hide, hide from whatever the next day has in store, out of sight. We never know what is around the corner. Everything seems more resolvable in the illuminated blackness, but time still rushes past. Daytime lurks around the corner, waiting.

The city at night is full of wonder and possibility, but it isn't enough. It isn't the answer. But what's the question?

I realise I have a headache, a dull thumping at my temples.

It's like a riddle. The story has become about what the story is about.

Waiting at the platform for the train to arrive, I lean back against a wall, frowning. There is a large advert on the opposite platform with trees and nature and it occurs to me that if the city can be so different by night, so would a forest. I could close the circle and return there. It will be like fulfilling a premonition.

I might not be getting any closer to finding the missing something that I'm seeking. But you never know what is around the corner.

The lights of the train, as it comes into sight, are too bright. I shield my eyes. They remind me of something I want to forget. My whole head hurts now. As the train draws into the platform, its wheels and brakes screech and whine, echoes of their arrival ringing in my ears.

The Colour

It was a colour that caused the misery.

I had been holidaying at the beach, Mexico – Lord knows I'd deserved it, propping up a desk five and a half days a week. But it wasn't to be.

Some say the location of Mexico is adversely affected – the hole in the sky draws the nightmare into its wake.

And I stared into the visions of the sky. It could happen to anyone – just like a freak plane crash, or a disease, or all manner of less than coincidental afflictions and occurrences.

I had been lying on the beach, as I say. I'd just been congratulating myself on such a good choice of vacation venue when the sky began to crimson – unless I'd fallen asleep for several hours, the heavens shouldn't have been colouring like this in mid-afternoon.

I searched the coastline for an explanation. I noticed fellow beachgoers eyeing the surrounding sands, water, mountain range for the cause.

Then the colour had gone.

So we thought – all returned to normal, but for the lingering memory upon the backs of our eyes of a reddening, deep reddening of the sky.

I thought fiddle-faddle to it. Who cared about the local oddities of the countryside, the ocean sky in this part of the world? I'd paid for flight, warmth. Not science.

I took to rubbing sun oil luxuriously into my skin. Never could be too careful with hotter temperatures.

When the screaming noise scorched through one ear and out of the other... ... ... in a high-pitched, nuclear whistle surely only dogs should detect.

The sea washed in the same as ever.

Nothing had changed, but I sat up and clutched my head in agony.

"What the hell was that?" I mumbled.

A migraine now blanketed my brain. A red blindness throbbed above my eyes.

In a single moment, I thought of strong beer, of chocolate biscuits, of my dog waiting patiently in his kennels on the other side of the world – I don't know why but that was what I thought of in my last moment of sanity for several hours.

I cried out. But this time I was alone.

I sensed the eyes of other tourists turn on me. Then the blur of colour evaporated into nothingness, leaving only its footprint on my memory.

In its place the sound returned.

Oh, Mother of God, my brain was on fire. I wrenched at my hair. Burning, frying – this was not good, this was not good.

My brain was smouldering. I wouldn't have been surprised if there had been smoke seeping from my ears.

Quickly, I was on my feet. I ran halfway down to the sea's edge. What good would that do? I ran back to my towel – token of a misplaced life of reason and rhyme, so it appeared.

The heat had gone. It had gone but the Fear had not.

How was it that I had the objectiveness of mind to observe separate and distinct reactions of people? One kind hastened away from this madman, gathering up books and plastic bottles, towels and mats – didn't want to leave them behind – others, the few, approached me with obvious fear, wanting to extend helping hands, totally at a loss for how to help. Could not blame them.

"I'm okay, I'm okay," I cried. Why say such a thing? Peculiar behaviour.

Yet the truth was that the colour had gone – for the time being at least – and the sound, dreadful screaming gush of noise, that had gone too.

What was I supposed to do? Go back to lying on the beach, wait for one or the other to reappear? Go and drink a brandy to steady myself?

I wished I had a friend to console me. To explain what had gone on.

?

Still, I did go back to my hotel room, buying water on the way. I hurried, despite the intense heat, which made me sweat badly – along with the strange trauma – made me sweat.

I had paracetamol in my room, and I drew the curtains and lay down in the shade of an air-conditioned room. Sleep soon took over and I ended up awakening when darkness had settled on the world.

I could hear the couple in the next room going at it hammer and tongs: "Ungh, ungh, ungh."

My headache hadn't gone and I didn't giggle to myself as I might have done on another night.

"Ungh, ungh, ungh, ungh."

I stood up from the bed, shakily, and was making my way towards the now half-empty bottle of water on top of the chest of drawers when it hit me, rifling through me the worst so far.

The previous time, that had been nothing but a premonition, an 121choed121er.

The redness came back, all bloated with pink and yellow and white, swirling, twisting, writhing into varying shades. But I didn't see it.

It came into my ears. Could hear the colour screaming into my ear, whistling through my head. Again, again, scream, screech, scream.

I sank to my knees in the centre of the room.

I probably screamed in pure horror. …How would I not have done? …Lurched to the closet, reasoning with addled logic that I could lock myself inside the cupboard and that way shut out the sound of the colour of the sound of the colour.

So I grabbed the closet door and pulled it open. And found myself looking down into a box. That's correct: I had pulled open the door and I was gazing not into a cupboard but downwards into a box.

I slammed it shut and fell backwards onto my backside like a drunken child.

The colour ripped through my senses – most of all

through my brain – with unrelenting force. I was a writing mass on the hotel room floor. But I didn't scream any more. …Could not produce a sound. …Could not pray for salvation. …Only knew one thing – the noise in my head.

There, upon the wall, I now saw signs – some kind of marks. They were *Y* shapes with a flat line across the top that made a triangle of the upper half.

Glimmering there in thin white, like luminous engravings in the dark room.

They meant nothing to me – nothing I could remember, at any rate. I imagined they must be some secret potenders of disconsolation …Tears came to my eyes as I looked at them. And had it not been for the screaming agony in my head, I would certainly have sat down and wept.

I didn't question where they had come from, at the time. I crawled to the door. I tried to avert my eyes, sought not to look at these symbols of forlornness, but my eyes were pulled towards them as though I craved them. I couldn't look away.

Because I could not look away, I fumbled with the door handle for what seemed an hour before it would open.

But open it did. And after a further hour, so it seemed, I could wrench my vision from the enlightening, endarkening marks on the wall, shimmering, swaying.

I looked through the doorway. It had opened, yes, but my senses misted and tumbled from side to side like an alcoholic on a ship in a storm. Retching again and again, I wanted to throw up my guts for eternity. *I was strong*, I told myself with some far away, friendly voice in my deepest psyche. I threw myself out of the door, immediately stumbled against the wall opposite.

The sickness had grown stronger. I could feel it in my bones, in my blood and in my skin. I felt possessed.

I slid down the wall like a squashed fly, slumped on the red carpet of the corridor.

A voice beckoned me, "Come, come, into the room, there is more to learn – to understand understand…"

And I staggered back to my feet. I was tossed to the

wall on the other side of the hallway. I thrust myself further away from the magnetic pull of the entrancing symbols inside the room. I stumbled with a dull thud against the wall once more.

Somebody appeared. Words beginning to form.

"You stupid idiot. Can't you…"

But sensing all was not well, the stumpy, middle-aged man drew back in fright, back from his own doorway into the safety, perhaps, of his room, where maddened, frightening men did not worm intoxicated with wells of insanity mirrored in their eyes.

"Jesus," I heard somewhere.

It echoed – echoed – 123choed – in my washing machine head – rumbling, thrown tumbling, bubbling and seething and coagulating. Echoed. Choed.

The end of the hall was near to me now. I stretched out a hand. Shiver and shudder, my backbone a thrashing snake.

I couldn't make out the staircase that ought to have been there, taking me down to the lobby, front desk, help. It should've been there of course. Though I'd forgotten such a rationality in my state.

No stairs. At the end of the corridor lay nothing but a drop. The carpet ended and deep redness the colour in my ears trailed away below.

I drew back.

Ahead and below stretched the colour, the noise. Smell of oranges and lemons – it was a good smell. I stood. I turned. Had to go past the room to get to the other end and the hopefully surviving other staircase. Didn't want to go as far as the door of my room, but had to.

The alarmed neighbour had remained, peering out of his door. His face like a shrunken head. His body up next to me no sense, it was five doors down but I could touch him if I wanted, but head so small.

"Oranges and lemons, the bells of St Clement's," I sang, a true maniac, smelling that delicious, tormenting odour again. "Here comes the chopper… chop off your head," I continued.

"Curiosity killed the cat, you know?" I shouted at the man, half-hiding behind his door. Further down the hall, others had assembled in cowardly positions of like him. I could not see that they were human; they were natural and afraid, not crazed like me.

I wanted to hurt them, bludgeon them repeatedly with blades, mutilate their watching faces. ...I knew no sense. This was not me, that's all I can say now.

But I did nothing, intent on passing the room.

The far end of the corridor was identical to the first, with a sheer drop of churning bright colour inviting and enveloping all.

I must have had an ounce of sanity not to give in immediately. Instead, I tore myself along the hallway and back to the first drop; then back to the second; first; second; latter; former, other. There was a greater number of scaredy cat faces along the lines of the tunnel but it wasn't a tunnel it was a corridor seemed a tunnel. Don't know which end of the hall it was that I finally stopped at, after running, running up and down – nor does it matter.

Something was wrong, oh something was wrong. That, I knew. And that it wouldn't get better.

When better a time to jump from the edge?

With only one look over my shoulder at the misshapen faces I wanted to murder, I plunged – with barely an ounce of sense left to drive me onwards – into the crimson abyss.

The white symbols from the bedroom wall branded my eyeballs, flying at me as I tumbled and fell, hurtling, my scream receding behind me.

You know that I survived.

People, including friends, say that I haven't been the same since that time – the accident, as they refer to the oddity from the sky, my haunting colour. I was scooped from the carpet of the lobby by the reception staff on night watch. Taken by ambulance, raging and roaring through Mexican streets with a swirling, whirling scream-screeching siren on its roof. My head was cracked. People like to see the scar. It divides the crown of my head into two distinct segments, west and east.

...I must have tangled with the banister of the stairs, they say, thud bump tumbled headfirst down the long flight of stairs – which were always there and had never gone away, I am assured.

The hospital was white, and though dirty I didn't complain. None the wiser as to what the fuck had taken me in its evil clutches, nevertheless I lived.

And I recovered, ugly scar a souvenir of the strange little war that had caught me up in its whirlwind of no-sense.

At length I could fly home, and then return to work.

Unsurprisingly, I have avoided holidays since that time. I spend my time quietly with simple hobbies. I warn people not to go to Mexico – too close to that hole in the sky, after all, I tell them.

My life fell back into its safe little groove – and I wasn't to be heard complaining.

Then once... just once... while working at my computer in the safety of my study, in the safety of a suburban house on the edge of London, I saw them again...

...those all-knowing white Symbols...

...I looked up from the keyboard and beheld a screen covered with blurred figures –the self-same as in that hotel. Disembodied from any sense, they floated there in a sky of crimson, swirling hypnotic, pure, deep red like the sky that time. There was a fire-coloured scream in my ears. It was so faint, so distant and so brief that I couldn't be sure if it had existed at all.

I cried out – must've closed my eyes – and the symbols were gone when my eyeballs alighted once more on the screen.

They brought no terror or doom in their wake.

And it's been okay. My life continues. If it was a flashback or not that brought those images to my home, I have no clue. I just hope.

Finding the Plot

Nine o' clock: Temple at Night

Seya Ward, Yokohama

I turn off the main road into the silent back streets, then take the path up to the temple.

I'm looking forward to finding solitude at the top of the hill. I plan to sit motionless in the pitch black and savour my surroundings. As I begin climbing the steep slope, a chill runs up my spine, as though I am entering forbidden territory. I always seem to feel unwelcome, as if I'm entering a sacred space that I shouldn't. There seems no logic to this.

The cemetery with its stone blocks of various shapes and sizes embedded in the ground appears on my left and, without knowing why, I find my breathing becomes tense. I can't look at the little shrines I had thought so beautiful on my last visit. The night-time certainly changes things. Just a perfunctory glance to my left and then I quicken my pace and don't look sideways.

I have never seen a ghost and I don't want to. If anyone sees me walking amongst the departed at this time of night, they will think I am a ghost. Perhaps they're right.

My grandmother, the sort of person who instantly understands people, was once fetching a night time glass of water when, standing at the sink, through the window she saw a pale, old woman walking in the garden. Rather than shrieking in terror or calling the police, she immediately knew, she later told me, that the elderly lady she beheld simply missed the garden that had once been hers and so she'd returned at night, when people wouldn't normally be around. She was matter-of-fact about it, simply accepting what she'd seen.

The charcoal sky above the cemetery might be filled with the spirits of the dead and buried, for all I know. Though I can't see them, perhaps they see me. Vaguely shimmering, floating, a few metres over my head in the tops of the trees and amongst the bamboo grove behind the graves? Would they wear insane smiles, trapped here, unable to move on, held back by some memory that haunted them, or some secret that they had searched for and never found in their lifetime?

Would they live out their days again and again, going through the same cycle of time, day and night, wandering the old, familiar places, hungry for some detail, wanting some resolution. I look across at the stone tombs and wonder if the ghosts are standing there amongst them.

Leaving the little cemetery behind me, I walk through the gate of the temple grounds and stop, my eyes trying to pick their way through the murky night. I can hardly make out the features of the walls and windows that I could see so clearly by day. I have that same feeling of being an intruder, snooping around private sites at night.

I never seem to feel as though I belong.

The black fog of night envelops the sleeping temple. I feel panic rising in me, but I don't know why. Maybe it is the ghosts further back down the hill. Despite the cold night, my face is hot and I'm sweating. I have the sensation that I am being watched but there is nobody around, not that I can see. I find myself thinking of the strange metal casket I had see in the cemetery and wonder if they have buried it yet. Odd for it to be lying there in the open like that. Whose was it? I seem to have forgotten how to breathe and have to do it deliberately. I force myself to inhale more slowly but I can't seem to fill up my lungs.

I remember my grandmother's calm acceptance of what she saw. I think of my grandfather and the memory of him, humorous and ever calm, a game of cards here, a sneaky glass of brandy together there, brings me a measure of calm.

In fact, I think of him every day. I had always assumed I would see him again – and then he was gone, just like that. The morning that he died, I was about to step into the shower when I smelled his aftershave. I didn't use aftershave. It put me in mind of him. That was peculiar, I thought. And later that day, I found out that he had gone. When I was told the news, I remembered that I had dreamt of him, too, the previous night.

I miss him a lot.

Now, with the memory, I feel strong again. I leave the temple grounds and with a set jaw, hurry back past the bamboos sloping away in the haunting black air, past the deathly, all-too-real stone blocks, past that steel coffin, buried or not, and find myself safely back at street level, no longer haunted, no longer haunting.

The Coffin Returns

The second time it happened, when the terror had subsided into mere panic, he lay there in the dark confines, mind spinning. A bead of sweat slowly rolled, like Japanese wartime torture, from his temple to the back of his head. Another droplet tickled his face and made its way to the back of his jaw bone, and in his fevered mind the thought arose that when that droplet collected and dripped from him onto the steel bed, that was when his time would run out,

,

,

,

...and all the while, there was the all-consuming desire to move his legs and arms, to roll on his side, but there was no space, he was constricted, constrained, shouting at the lid above him, just like before. The words seemed to echo before he'd even finished uttering them, rebounding into his face. Hot tears of rage joined the hot beads of perspiration. And he even laughed, like a madman, at the recollection of his recent conversation with his doctor.

"You need to consider your sleep hygiene."

"Sleep hygiene?"

"Is your room dark? You need to sleep in a dark place."

"It's fairly dark."

"Do you have black-out curtains?"

"Er... no."

"You'd be surprised how the slightest light on an electrical device or a crack of light at a doorway will affect the quality of your sleep."

"I see."

"Is it quiet in your bedroom?"

"It could be quieter. There's a lot of traffic – you know, buses, cars, on the main road round the corner."

Doctor Hare smiled benignly. "Are your windows double-glazed?"

"Well, no."

"If you could get them double-glazed, you'd be amazed at the difference it might make to your sleep."

Nat frowned. There was no way that he could afford double-glazing or blinds. He was living hand to mouth, with the cost of living and his poorly paid job.

"Consider it," said Doctor Hare. "And lastly – and this is a must – you must have a quiet wind-down routine – no excitement, no adrenalin. Turn down your lights, meditate, think nice thoughts."

"Think nice thoughts?"

"Absolutely."

Doctor Hare smiled from ear to ear. He had no cares in the world.

And here he had found perfect darkness, a blackness that the artist Kazimir Malevich would have cherished – and probably claimed ownership of; after all, he had painted his Black Square long before Nat had wound up trapped inside an unburied coffin.

And it was a very good alternative to double-glazed windows. Dr Hare would've been proud.

…But on the adrenalin part of the equation, he was failing. His heart was slamming against his ribs so hard that he found it even harder to breathe than it already was in these claustrophobic walls.

His thoughts were not nice.

When he was small, he'd had a pet – in the loosest sense of the word. He could also have said that it was a prisoner. He had kept it in a little matchbox. Thoughtfully he had put some grass in the matchbox, and regularly he'd drop teardrops of water into the box from a glass. At first, he was vigilant. He'd give it water more often than it needed. He'd change its grass. He'd catch tiny insects and feed them to him, unaware of what dragonflies ate. And the dragonfly was seemingly content; he didn't struggle much, but for the occasional frenzied vibration of wings.

No-one could blame him for keeping this little pet-prisoner. Its beauty was so great, its colours shining like a psychedelic truth, its odd shape like a poetic dream of a biplane. It would be impossible to let it fly away, its joyfulness forgotten. He may have been no more than six years old, but he knew the fleetingness of life. Perhaps because his parents had died before the age of memory, he had a heightened sense of the illusion of the egg timer: the sand does not slip from the top jar to the bottom one; slips out of sight and memory altogether.

So like a jealous god, he fenced in his dragonfly and stole glances at it, careful that it didn't escape. And like a careless God, with time he paid less attention to it. The water supply was less frequent. The hopeful nutrition was scarce. The chaotic beating of its wings fell on deaf ears, like a tree falling in a forest where no human foot falls, like the infamous zen one hand clapping.

A strange conclusion to his brief experiment as zookeeper: two weeks after trapping the insect, he entered his bedroom, toys on his mind. Something made him think of his little pet. He started to cross the room to the desk to open the matchbox that sat there, but it was already ajar. Something was making a faint tapping noise and his eyes travelled to the window. At the corner of the room, there was the dragonfly, flying again and again in desperation at the window.

Feeling ashamed, he opened the window, cognizant that he should put an end to this. The dragonfly was quick to seize its opportunity; but as it drifted out of the window, it stuttered and fell, a war plane struck by flak from below, its engine on fire, smoke bellowing out of its fuselage. Once, twice, it tried to correct its course.

Nat didn't see what became of it. With a frown, he opened his toy box, but it was difficult to concentrate. Once, he glanced at the half-open matchbox, then went and took it and dropped it into the dustbin.

And half-conscious in the coffin, the recollection came to him.

This might be karma. Perhaps dragonflies did matter, after all.

Perhaps he was God's plaything.

Perhaps God had got bored and found other toys to entertain himself with, while Nat lay languishing in his matchbox on the side of the hill, darkness outside the box, darkness inside the box, darkness inside his head.

Like before, God or surreal fate or physical laws as yet unknown relented and a hopeless push at the lid saw it give way.

Somehow he found the strength to climb out.

The absence of sound at the top of the hill gushed through his ears and into his thoughts, belying the din of the town centre not far away. His eyes struggled to adjust to the thick darkness amongst the surrounding sea of trees.

This time he forced himself to touch his tormentor, check he was not dreaming, that this was real life. He touched cold metal with a single finger, half-anticipating a shock of volts that didn't come. Only the same cold and unforgiving texture he had lain inside, locked helplessly inside.

For a few eternal seconds, he stood before it, as motionless as the walls of metal themselves. He could only stand still, mind not working, limbs redundantly awaiting instruction.

As the beginnings of logic returned to him, he understood that *Kafkaesque* didn't mean something that just happened in between the covers of a book.

He stumbled home, unlocked the front door which he felt like he hadn't seen for a week, and crashed into bed after two minutes, barely stopping to neck a few slugs of brandy. He slept in the deep cloudy waters of drunkenness, and denial, waking up at exactly 11:10.

Sunlight was clawing at a gap in the curtains. He thought of Dr Hare and his benign smile and innocence. Nat lay there, trying to put back together the fragments of the night before for a few seconds before choosing instead the bliss of denial.

He knew that at some point he had to face his fears.

Remembering, his heart began to beat faster with fear – dread that if he approached the coffin, it would somehow lure him inside and enclose him helplessly. Nevertheless, he got dressed, swallowed a coffee and set off for the hill where it lay.

Back in the hillside cemetery, he hovered over it, still grimacing as though it might reach out to grab him. It seemed new, polished and somehow pure. What the fuck was a coffin doing here, above the ground? They belonged firmly beneath the surface, for God's sake, well out of sight and unable to get you in their grasp.

Sunlight glinted through the trees and reflected blindingly off the surface. There were no markings of any kind. It was impersonal.

Seeing it did nothing to quell his turbulence. He knew that he had to look inside. First, he checked right and left, wanting for some reason to be quite alone. No-one was nearby, although in a house overlooking the graveyard there was the shape of a woman in the window. He knew that she was watching him because she moved carefully and slowly out of sight, almost imperceptibly, too craftily to be coincidence.

Using both hands, he lifted the lid. Easily, smoothly, it yawned open until it almost stood at a rectangle, but not quite, bent slightly forward as if shielding its contents. But there were no contents, apart from the unthinkable memories of the night before that were encapsulated within the four silver walls.

Its interior was all metal, exactly like the outside. It was less shiny, but the same steely colour and smooth texture. He ran his hand over the floor in horrified awe, as if touching a valuable, fragile sculpture or a priceless painting. He couldn't make any sense of it. He couldn't fathom why it was here, let alone why he had woken up inside the hideous thing in the middle of the night. Absolutely man-made and new, it rested ill-at-ease with its surroundings: the natural brown and green of the trees, the faded, worn headstones partially hidden behind long grass and moss. The odd little graveyard, if it could qualify as such with its few graves, seemed dirty and forgotten in its presence; and vice-versa, the coffin was ugly here, like a peculiar piece of industrial garbage or scrap metal in a pretty wood.

He felt helpless. No wonder he had preferred denial. What was he supposed to do? What do you do when Kafka comes knocking?

He returned to the main road using a different route, continuing down to the bottom of the grassy slope and taking a winding path through more trees back to the noise and smoky gas of constant traffic.

He paused, looking back in disbelief at the wooden fence and trees behind it which obscured the miniature graveyard. He wouldn't have even known it existed.

Nat shook his head and returned home in a daze, oblivious of the faces and conversations of passers-by, unaware of the sunshine and clear blue sky. At home, he sat for an hour without so much as fixing himself a drink. He stared at the floor, at the low table, as if they might reveal an answer to him, an explanation. They told him nothing, however. There wasn't a rational basis for analysing the matter. He couldn't think of any options at all and had no choice but to wait, however uneasily, and see. Even outside of the coffin, he was within its authority.

He was due to visit his grandmother in the hospital and quickly got ready. Walking to the train station, he glanced unhappily in the direction of the trees on the small hill beyond the main road.

He was soon on the train and it was good to be away from home, to leave it all behind, tainted with puzzling, troubling memories of nights of horror. He had bought a newspaper in the station and now let himself become involved in the far-off reports of tragedy, the football stories and the decisive opinions of the editor about what exactly was wrong with everything. The pages and pages of clear black and white print enveloped him like waves of escape. By the time the train arrived, he had partially managed to drive his own problems out of his head. He focused on seeing his grandmother, and took the bus to the hospital, as it was waiting there outside the station, instead of taking a taxi.

In the hospital, he strode leisurely along the corridor, the sheer whiteness of everything suggestive of an image of heaven, but such a picture at once dissolved by the stench of chemicals masking the smell of rotting flesh and disease. Nat wore his most cheerful mask as he passed the wards to left and to right. The last thing the patients in those rooms wanted was to see an anxious face scurrying past. Weary expressions and looks of consternation watched him pass.

He came to the end of the corridor, turned and opened a door onto two scowling nurses spitting insults at each other in hushed tones. They glared at him with a mixture of guilt and reproach and he apologized and retraced his steps. More wards, with six old women occupying them in various states of consciousness. Near the end of the last corridor, his eyes fell on a tall thin woman, some seventy years old, propped up in her small bed.

"Mummy. Mummy," she bawled like a small child in unbearable pain. Nat was sure that he had never heard such a heartbreaking cry in all his life. It poured out pure despair. At the same time, his heart was chilled by the pitiful sound, not to mention the indignity of the old woman who could do no more than cry out. He hurried on, angry that his grandmother should be confined to such a place. Between tears, the plea followed him as he hurried on:

"Mummy!"

A nurse rushed past him in the opposite direction, no doubt on her way to quieten the unhappy patient.

Rooms of equipment, busy, efficient nurses at a desk, and finally he came to the last room on the left. He saw the familiar face of his grandmother, looking all alone, and Nat dismissed the frenzy of other thoughts from his mind, feeling like a child again, remembering gardens, school, churches and humour in an instantaneous pot-pourri of senses. Thoughts of the open green sea came, and of the little bungalow where he had grown up, and childhood hopes and fears. Two funerals were always close on the heels of memory when he saw his grandmother; she would have been devastated to know that and he hid it from her.

She felt his presence now and looked up with delighted eyes.

"Hello," she said in a cheerful but croaky voice as he approached the bed. Her eyes betrayed the pain, but as always she kept a brave face fixed in place. She could have been a saint, so peaceful and contented despite the situation.

He looked at her and a smile crept into his lips.

"How are you, Nan?" he asked.

"Oh, not too bad," she said with that London twang she had spent a lifetime denying. Nat sat down on the edge of the bed, kissing her on the withered skin of her cheek, still surprised after all this time that it wasn't as smooth as it had been when he had been growing up.

"You've got lots of flowers." He glanced appreciatively at the pinks, reds and yellows on the shelf behind and the plastic table next to her. He thought how nicely they brightened the stark whiteness of the ward. With unease, he surveyed the patients sharing the room with her and realised that they were all very old. She wouldn't like that, preferring younger company. Nat nodded politely to them and smiled, though only an anxious lady next to the window seemed to notice and said,

"Hello. Funny weather we're having."

He nodded.

In comparison to his grandmother, the others looked jaded and hopeless, barely moving and, when they did, only in slow motion like ancient turtles. He was probably biased, his mind full of memories of a younger woman always involved in something - church fairs, charity work or sending Nat off to school.

"So when are you going home?" he asked as she ran her hand through his hair, as if to check if he was real or not.

"Well, I don't know really. They haven't told me much. I feel a lot better, but I do get tired. And I'll have to come back, I suppose, to check it's all worked out okay."

He nodded gravely.

"So how about you? How's your life in the big city?" There she went, as usual, Nat thought with annoyance that he couldn't help – redirecting attention away from herself every time, even though it was her well-being was at stake; she must truly have believed that she didn't matter, God would take care of everything.

He smiled. "I'm fine."

He recalled the coffin and realised that he was lying, he wasn't fine, but put it out of his mind.

"I'll talk to the doctors – find out when you can go home," he said. "I expect you'll have to take it easy with the gardening at first."

She smiled at this.

"And no more running into cars."

She chuckled, and the chuckle turned into a cough that wracked her lungs for some time. Nat began to see the impact of the accident on her physical condition, broken hip aside. Once again he silently cursed the incompetent fool who had all of a sudden reversed into her from a parked position, ramming her to the ground. At her age, the shock alone must have had a destructive effect on her body.

"What've you been up to then?"

Again the morbid encounter with a coffin came first to Nat's mind along with an unpleasant flash of recollection.

She peered more searchingly at him as he hesitated.

"Working hard," he answered lamely.

Her eyes smiled proudly. "As usual."

So much hard work and so many drunken nights, he considered.

"Yes, you know. The usual routine," he laughed, remembering the long hours he had put in first during his schooldays and then for the degree which he had funded by serving two-for-one pizzas on the Broadway.

"You're happy though, are you love?" she asked, her large, grey eyes growing very serious.

"Yes," he lied, without hesitation.

"And you'll be thinking about getting yourself a nice girlfriend soon, or have you already got one? A handsome fellow like you," she added with a cheeky smile.

Nat held up his hands as though to keep this threat at bay. "Unfortunately, you're the only one who thinks so, Nan." He grinned self-consciously.

"Nonsense. And are you managing to go to church?"

The question had taken Nat unawares. He opened his mouth to speak but failed to lie about this one.

"You must try and go, love," she advised him kindly. It was for his own good, that was all.

"Yes, absolutely. I do try," he improvised.

Maybe he could get an exorcism that would banish the coffin from his life.

A melancholy smile came to her lips.

"But as I said, you know, it has been so busy," Nat added.

"Well, try and go at least from time to time." Her tone was almost reprimanding him now. "There's a church near you, isn't there?"

Nat struggled to remember where his nearest church was, and wondered who went there in this day and age, but he couldn't think under the pressure of her saintly gaze.

"Oh, yes," he assured her weakly.

She looked at the pendant handing around his neck.

"You're still wearing that thing," she said.

"Yes, I am," he smiled patiently.

"I don't like it at all, that medallion. How about getting a nice cross instead, eh? It'll protect you."

"It's not a medallion, Nan, and I like it. It has meaning for me."

She shrugged. "Well, I'm not sure what it mcans," he complained. He let it go without trying to explain.

He could vividly picture the old grey church of his boyhood, standing proudly, defiantly, opposite the multi-storey car park and the roundabout by the shopping mall. He could still smell the incense, its grey and velvet scent. He could see himself walking through the foyer with his grandmother piously leading the way, into the serene, hushed dimness.

His grandmother too began to reminisce, recollecting the people they had known, the outings they had been on, and how good a boy Nat had been. He let her think aloud, enjoying the sight of her brightening eyes with each old face that entered her mind, every favourite service that she called up. He blocked out the renewed cries of the howling woman down the corridor and as they talked about old times fell to wondering, as he had before now, if she couldn't somehow have stayed where she was, living in the village near the sea where she had known everyone.

But money had run out, and when Nat had left home for university, she had declared proudly that she needed a change and moved to a small flat in a town just far enough for her to lose touch with old friends, though some did visit, and for her not to be able to see the sea without a long bus journey. He thought of the financial strain that she must have had in seeing him safely through school, with his parents gone.

"I always knew you'd be a good lawyer," she was telling him.

"You did always say that," he smiled.

"Oh, yes," she echoed, "I always said that."

"And you were a brilliant Falstaff in the school play. Outshone the others."

"Nan, I forgot half my lines!"

"Well that made everybody laugh, and it was only on the first night, anyway," she said, undeterred. "It was lovely."

He was the star in her show, just like all children were for their parents or guardians.

Nat noticed the tiredness creeping over her face. In fact, not only her. It was washing over Nat as well. The previous night had been a living nightmare, after all.

It was getting harder to ignore the noise of the desperate patient. He felt less tolerant than before. Couldn't they do something for her? Those bickering nurses in their little room with their little grievances.

"You look tired now," he said. He glanced at the plastic

tube hooked to her weak-looking arm, studied the metal bars at the side of the bed, there for safety's sake but seeming to trap her there.

Were we all trapped, in some way?

"I'll be all right."

He rested his hands on the rail and was reminded of the smooth, cold metal of the coffin. The image crawled to the forefront of his mind, impossible to ignore. He had to think about leaving. He was finding it harder to hold it all together.

There came a particularly blood-curdling wail from the troubled woman. The sound of it had a profound effect on Nat.

"Jesus," he said, forgetting himself. It was taking all his effort to be cheerful for his grandmother, block out that woman's noise and resist the urge to scream himself from the strange events that had happened to him. "Can't they help her?"

His grandmother was asleep.

It dawned on him that the woman calling for her mother was screaming in much the same way he had the previous night, both afraid of dying a premature death, alone. Wasn't it always premature, though? In his mind's eye, he glimpsed the coffin, ugly because of its strange location, and at the same time, he had no idea why, in some way cathartic and pure; well, that didn't make any sense at all. He recalled banging on the lid with his hands, beating the sides of the coffin with fists, writhing and kicking inside the morbid box, sensing that he was already slowly suffocating…

The confinement. The choking stale air and the confusion.

The uselessness: his oppressor, the solid, ingeniously designed metal, too strong.

Finally pathetically pushing at the lid out of habit. It giving way.

Open.

Daytime in the hillside graveyard, the trees dancing

menacingly above as he gasped in lungfuls of clean air. Strengthless, scrambling clear.

As he recalled the memory, so vivid, his grandmother's eyes slowly opened and she gazed into his with a look that wasn't so pure; it was sanctimonious. He looked away. She fell back to sleep, looking peaceful.

The light in the hospital ward hurt his eyes. He remembered the morning sun as he'd emerged from his claustrophobic hell – unnaturally yellow and blinding, his eyes so tired that they made the sunlight flicker. Here, the hospital strip lights did the same, flickering and sickening him. They seemed brighter than before. The sickly white smell of hygiene wafted into his nose. The howling woman had been calmed; it was quiet now.

He kissed his grandmother on the cheek and left the room.

At the vending machine near the lifts, he bought a plastic cup of weak coffee, struggling to raise it to his lips for the trembling of his hand. He felt sick.

He thought of his grandmother's grey eyes and how they had suddenly looked at him with judgement. He remembered the shape of a woman in a house near the cemetery, looking at him.

Perhaps she had seen something. Perhaps she could help. Perhaps she knew something.

The unreal whiteness of the hospital appeared yellower now. As he waited for the lift, one strip light flickered on and off, as if it too was sick. The whole creamy off-white colour of the place resembled decaying flesh.

It was a relief to emerge into the sunny blue air of the car park, breathing normally again – in much the same way he had done when he had burst from the ethereal black gloom of the coffin a short time before.

He stood up from the round table and chair. Standing alone in the centre of his living room, they resembled the apparatus for a séance. He was tired. His body was pulling his spirit towards unconsciousness. Perhaps it was the other way around. Every one of his muscles was on the verge of sleep.

He went into the bedroom and studiously avoided the bed in the corner, walking to the sliding window that led out to the narrow balcony. It was pitch black outside. He gazed back at the bed and then went to sit outside.

He had a premonition that it would happen again tonight. He couldn't say why but he could sense it coming.

What if he didn't sleep? He went and sat in the dark night air and began to wait.

Something moved in the black gloom beyond the balcony, down on the ground. It could have been a tramp hiding out amongst the machinery and heaps of earth and building materials that were gathered to build new houses for new happy families. It might feasibly have been a burglar surveying his target in preparation for later on that night. He heard a second movement further to the right, followed by a childish shriek.

"That's not the right way to do it. You do it like this," a child's voice cried with the pompousness young boys brandish in their own infinite world.

"That's what I did, Marvey!" complained a younger voice.

"No, you didn't," the expert retorted. "You don't know what you're doing. You don't know the word." He scoffed in disdain.

Nat rolled his eyes as he listened.

They were climbing up onto a digger, which had been left in the middle of the muddy upheaval. Nat could just about make out two tiny, agile shapes clambering gleefully in and around the cabin of the machine, unaware that they were being watched. It didn't seem a safe playground. There were gaping trenches dotted around the open expanse of land. There must have been rocks and stones to stumble into and trip over. He peered uneasily into the darkness, wondering whether to shout a warning. After five minutes of play, however, they got bored and disappeared into the night, only echoes now haunting the sky they left behind.

Nat wondered if he had been that untroubled in his childhood? He remembered nightmares of another, unfamiliar world visiting him from time to time. He had awoken from those terrified, still seeing the misshapen, elongated faces laughing at him in the dark. The people in that world were in a different perspective that transcended reality; they were far away from him but at the same time he could reach out and touch them. At the age of seven or eight, he had dreaded a night filled with those nightmares.

"Nan, will I have a *horrible*?" he had asked his grandmother.

"No, duck. You won't," she would assure him. And given her blessing, he hadn't. Unless he forgot to ask for her blessing. Then he might awake in terror, unable to make sense of the distorted visions.

And now?

What was the blessing that would keep away the current transcended reality?

What was the magic word that would keep him safe at night?

As a child, in his sleep, he would forget where things were and walk out of his bedroom, turn left and drift through the hall to his parents' room, turn left again, pushing open their wooden door, and go in to find comfort. And there was the double bed, huge, clean and unused as it had been for years – ever since their death. There he would stand in the strange room, moonlight coming through the windows where the curtains were always open. Their absence had blurred with his nightmare.

It had been as uncertain as the dream. Were they coming home later on? Then he would remember that no, they weren't.

Nat rested his head back against the window, looking at the black void of the sky with the same eyes that had beheld the unruffled bed where his parents should have been breathing the heavy sighs of sleep.

He never had known what to say. To best friends the truth was all right. To insensitive teachers and other kids, his father had done great things – been a spy, or a footballer or a painter. That strategy worked until they were all a little older and more practised in the art of cynicism.

Drunk, his father had crashed his car. Beyond that, the details of how it happened weren't known, although it was generally believed that he'd fallen asleep in a drunken stupor following an evening of overtime at his office job. The company had been under great pressure and as a result, so had he. Working an unhealthy amount of the time and drinking too much the rest, presumably endeavouring to forget all the work.

And like those who are most deeply in love, his mother hadn't been able to cope with the tragic fate. She felt she had expected too much of her husband. She felt to blame for not being there in the car. She thought that she should have been able to see it coming, should have been able to head it off.

She slipped into a morbid trance, unable to find the key to get out.

She had taken her own life.

She had walked into the sea.

His grandmother had said, between tears, that it was all for the best. His grandmother had been so strong.

He hadn't understood why, but now he remembered her words more clearly than their living faces. He'd been too young.

He recalled odd images only: like the one where he hid behind his mother as she visited a friend. They stood outside the front door chatting and she said about Nat,

"He's gone all shy. He's not usually this shy."

Had it ever happened at all? Could he trust his mind and his memories?

He remembered his father's ruddy, beleaguered face at the dinner table. But little more. And his grandmother had barely mentioned them before he was fifteen, for reasons of her own. Too painful perhaps.

His grandmother had been a strict Catholic and had taken him to church for the rest of his childhood to continue his conditioning. There he had felt restful in the dark and airy shadows behind thick pillars, kneeling on pews in communion with the supernatural and overawing power of the Church, its doctrines and strict mercy. Daunting images aside, it had been a sociable place. He had met new friends there for a while. He had got involved, became an altar server for a short time.

The bullying was something he had had the capacity to withstand. Some of the rougher, more worldly boys took a dislike to Nat. He was different. He said odd things. He went to a different school and it was posh – he must have been stuck up. He came to church with an old woman.

He wasn't cool. He was the perfect target. But all of that he could fight. When the red cassocks gathered above him in the sacristy began to punch and kick too hard, he would return a timely strike so that they backed off, cackling, to gather their collective wit for a time. It troubled him that they would differentiate and laugh at him for so little. But worse was his fear of the Father.

There was his own father, the drinker, who had turned wine into water and paid the price for it.

Then there was God the Father, who also had created Nat, and who was angry with him because of his sins. Nat was bad. Owing to Nat's evil ways, his Father had had to come to Earth and die, to pay the price for them. So it was Nat's fault. He had never quite clarified whether he was also responsible for his Dad's death. He couldn't ask his grandmother; she didn't much like to talk about things like that. But in his own thoughts, the two fathers and his guilt seemed enmeshed and it was confusing.

"You'll understand when you're older," she once said. "You're a smart boy, so you mustn't worry. You're a good boy, too."

Was he smart? Was he good? Surely, in fact, he was inherently bad? Something about Adam... He hadn't killed his mother, that much he knew. His Dad had kind of done that.

But Nat was sure that he himself had something to do with his Dad's death. They didn't say as much at church, but they did seem to hint at it. Something about a sacrifice.

"Judge not lest ye be judged." But there seemed to be a hell of a lot of judgements made at church, from Father O' Donovan, from the sacred Church laws and certainly from the other altar boys.

They said a lot of good things there too: stuff about love and kindness ...and heaven. And, during services, it was a haven from the world.

And there was one piece of advice that didn't come from church – his grandmother's mantra. Etched in his head were her words,

"Look your fears right in the face and they won't seem so bad."

When he went to the new school at eleven, before his first part-time job, before college ...whenever.

"And," she would add, "There's always a door marked *Exit*, so really there's nothing to worry about, duck."

He wasn't sure about that last part.

He gazed into the dark expanse of the construction site below. Out there were invisible graves dug up between the heaps of earth by mechanical yellow monsters with clawing arms, hollow pits into which errant kids might fall.

At both his father's, and then his mother's, funeral, Nat had stood in the cemetery near the sea at the front of the black-clad, mourning members of the family. Solemnity had hung in the air like the after-scent of sudden violence.

He remembered the second time, his mother's, as the coffin had been lowered into the earth, Nat had rushed away from his grandmother and the crowd to stand at the edge of the grave, looking far down at the polished brown lid. He could only have been staring into the pit for three seconds before he was pulled back, in danger of falling, but those seconds were long enough for the irrational notion to knock on the door of his mind: what if she's not dead? Nat, after all, had never seen her dead body. So went the irrational meditations of a small child.

On the balcony, tiredness was washing over Nat like the surf of the incoming tide. He shivered from sitting inactive for so long. He wanted to go inside and sleep. But the premonition remained. Tonight of all nights he was sure it would descend upon him.

He had to stay awake.

He watched television for several hours: wacky game shows with contestants laughing in ecstasy. He drank countless refills of coffee until he was sick of it. He had to sleep some time, he knew. If only he could make it to morning, though, he would feel protected by the light of day. And even if he wasn't, his chances of escape seemed better once the sun was up.

An ancient horror film came on at half past two. It was clumsy. At a hotel being used to shoot a horror film, a ghostly monster picked off guests. Despite the film's datedness, Nat was intrigued. The exaggerated television fear of each victim proved vaguely reassuring to him, and he didn't switch channel through hangings, hauntings and shootings. One of the cast was less than innocent; he knew something about what was going on. But he too bought his end, pulled hypnotically into a dirty grave. At this point, Nat switched over, wishing the last part hadn't happened. He watched leisurely golf, less than real in the silence of the night, but the image of the man falling into the grave seemed to have stained the screen; he could still see it, superimposed on the spotless putting greens and fairways.

Gradually the golf began to comfort him, to take his thoughts away again. Each shot was followed by a polite round of applause. Here was civilized life. The vast golf course was the Garden of Eden, where the players strolled contentedly from one smooth landscape to the next, their most pressing concern the demanding angle of the next shot. Nat was dreamily resolving to watch golf more often when he nodded off to sleep as he sprawled comfortably on the couch.

When he woke up, his heart was racing and he struggled to remember where he was, who he was. Should he go down the hall to his parents' room?

He rubbed his eyes, coming back to his senses in the bright overhead light of the room. He had dreamt of muddy graves in quiet corners of the golf course. He had tried to rejoin the throng of patient spectators, finding his way between ugly orange and yellow construction machines on the bright grass. Two children had mocked him. Now he stood up to switch on the lamp in the corner and turn off the glare above.

Sitting down again on the edge of the leather couch, it came to him that he was still safely here. Although he had failed to fight off the onslaught of sleep, he was unharmed. He was in his own home.

For a while he paced the room. He was grateful to have got away with a dose of rest, but he didn't dare return to sleep. Infuriating that he should be controlled by fear in this way. He only wanted to sleep normally, like everyone else.

He checked the television again. Only an ancient black and white romance on. It didn't look too bad, but he was sick of TV. He felt like moving. Turned it off and put on his trainers and raincoat, located a grey woollen hat in a drawer and pulled it on.

He would obey his grandmother's constant advice. He would go and stare in the face of his fear.

Soon he was walking between the sleeping houses in the direction of the main road, glad to be moving and no longer trapped in the television room.

The night air was cool. As he walked, he began to notice how weary he was. His eyes ached. The acrid aftertaste of coffee lingered in his mouth and he felt unclean and shabby.

But still he was glad to be moving. The streets were deserted at this early hour – until a man in a red tracksuit emerged from his house and passed Nat, jogging slowly in the opposite direction. He nodded at Nat as he went by. His eyes had deep circles beneath them and his face was drawn and yellow. Perhaps he too couldn't sleep.

Nat turned away from the main road, heading in the direction he was beginning to know so well. In the distance, the first early morning trains were beginning to rumble and creak into life.

He lit a cigarette and started up the hillside, leaving the sleeping, normal world behind, entering the realm of waking nightmares instead. This was a pilgrimage into hell. Once at the top of the hill, he looked to his left and spotted his inanimate nemesis, stock still and menacing a few metres away from the slope, away to his left.

An unseasonably icy breeze climbed in through the cracks of his coat and sweater. But the rest was the same. Dark evergreen wall of trees straight ahead, forbidding, concealing the unknown. Slope rolling away from him, hardly the place for the small headstones dotted on its side. It made him dizzy to look down at the casket where he had awoken, trapped, expecting to suffocate to death. The blood raced to his head, temples throbbed.

He couldn't feel his legs beneath him.

Was it the leaves on the ground? Something had moved, or had he imagined it?

There came a rippling crack, the booming sound of something large splitting apart that startled Nat like a slap across the face. A long, sinister rumble of thunder announced itself.

He was weak and mortal. Small. The headstones dotted around the slope seemed bigger than before. No rain came. Not yet. Only stillness, in the midst of which every tiny sound was amplified. He heard the drone of a car, far away. The leaves of the trees above fluttered. Something twitched in the grass.

He was aware of being far from the civilization. He was in some primal realm where modern logic didn't apply. More than that, he felt far from anyone he had ever known. The graveyard was as familiar as all graveyards, ever-present death.

Then he made himself absolutely still.

He had heard a whisper.

He waited, conscious of the amber glow at the tip of his cigarette, drawing malicious attention to him.

Whispering again? His imagination?

There could be madmen here. He hadn't thought of that. So foolish. Some new violence, as threatening as anything supernatural.

Now he couldn't hear anything. There was nothing but a morbid hush. A truck passed by on the road below, and Nat cursed it for disturbing his attention.

He heard sounds again but couldn't identify them. Memories of sounds stirred by the lorry? Or something real?

He no longer felt alone. Strange shapes formed in the darkness and in the shadows within it. Cast by the oblong moon above? Or by his mind? He took a step nearer to the coffin, ready to turn and flee at any moment.

Then he stopped dead in his tracks, body and heart grinding to a sickly halt at the hollow thumping noise that reached his ears. A dull thumping noise.

Followed by what was more of a knocking, almost polite. And then again more thumping of clenched fists.

Thunder again cracked open the sky. The promise of rain filled the air.

No, this was illusion, no more than a daydream conjured up by fevered imagination. No living person lay inside a coffin, nobody gasped for help.

Nat's mind.

The thunder retreated into the distance, into nothingness, fading out with only a small echo.

Silence again.

Muffled banging again.

A louder crackle of exploding thunder ripped open the clouds directly above his head.

He stood over the long, metal box, eyeing it in a frenzy, trying to work out what he could do. He had the opportunity to save some fellow prisoner. And to find another like himself!

Rain spattered his hair and clothes, and the grass and leaves. Thrown down from the fierce skies so hard that Nat was drenched in a matter of seconds, but oblivious to it, staring down at the coffin, his heart pounding against his ribs.

He tried to check his own sanity. Was the awful sound a figment of his deranged mind? Now he could hear nothing but the deafening roar of rain as it filled the vacuum of silence that had existed only just before. Thousands of hands scraping desperately, viciously at thin air, that was the sound of the rain.

It was hard to see properly. Water in his eyes, streaks of rain flashing in front of him, separating the coffin from his sight. He squinted down at the drops pounding the steel surface and disappearing as they ran down its side, others bouncing upwards, doing everything possible to deaden the noise that Nat thought he heard.

Awkwardly he put his fingers onto the rim of the box. He didn't want to touch it. But he had to. He wanted to turn and run as fast as he could back down the hill. But he forced himself to stay there.

No sound but the rain.

Then the thumping resumed, frantic, from inside. Nat heard the cries too. My God, he thought, why did I doubt my mind?

The voice was distant, drowned out by the filthy, psychopathic rain. A wailing cry, incoherent. As his rain-soaked fingers tried to gain leverage on the lip of the coffin's lid, he made out a simple plea, a stretched word without letters… It drifted away in the wind and rain.

His fingers, unaccustomed to hard, manual labour, pulled at the lid with no result.

He looked desperately around him, imagining amongst the trees the eyes of menacing witches peering from the edge of the copse, but it was a nightmare within a nightmare, morbid fantasy inside this grim reality.

"Please help me." The far-off cry of a small voice.

Nat was shouting. "I'm gonna get you out." He wanted to tell the victim to stay calm but the words were pointless and didn't leave his lips.

A moan – ghastly, a blood-curdling moan of loss. Such a pathetic sound. An image of the old woman in the hospital, crying out for her mother, came to him. Pitiful knocking followed – a slow-motion, underwater gesture. Nat felt bile rise inside him, found time to spit on the ground to stop himself from being sick.

Regaining his balance, he tore in fury at the lid. No movement. He tried again, with all of his force. Nothing. It was his turn to scream at the sky, fists clenched. He panted. He couldn't get in, could not move this lid. One of the pallbearers' handles on the side of the coffin scraped his shins. He wanted to pound on the lid with his fist but it could only alarm the trapped person inside, scare him more.

He knew he could go all the way back down the slope, along the road, and get a tool to come back and open the coffin. It might be too late by then. He could go and find a nearby house, seek help from there. But he didn't dare to leave.

He stood there panting, clothes wet through and droplets of water rushing down his face, neck and spine.

The hopeless thumping had stopped. Nat wretched again, fighting the urge to throw up all over the lid. His mind went blank. The situation, the rain drumming down, the lack of sleep... For a moment he felt faint.

Inside, somebody was gasping for air, soaked in sweat, skin crawling with fear, mind crawling with fear, in torturously slow seconds that could have been hours. Nat couldn't let himself give up on this new victim. He fought through his discomfort, his desire to run away and hide somewhere. *Look your fears right in the face and they won't seem so bad.* And there was always a door marked *Exit*, wasn't there?

He walked a few paces away, searching the ground for something that he'd seen. There, in the damp soil, he fished around amongst the few broken slabs of rock, finding the best weapon.

He marched back to the coffin.

He clenched his teeth.

"God help us!" he said, eyes closed, then opened and fixed them on one corner of the seam between lid and box. He planted his legs firmly in the soaked ground, used all of his body weight, all of his adrenalin, prized the narrow rock up and down. He went along the edge doing the same thing.

It seemed to be doing something.

Once, he slipped on the soaking grass but replanted himself and continued his efforts. The rain was less malicious than before but he was oblivious to it anyway. He no longer heard anything. Trancelike, he used every ounce of strength.

Finally, it moved.

His surroundings returned. Images flashed through his head. Who was in the coffin?

And in a different corner of his mind, he saw his grandmother, crows on a cliff, his parents' graves…

The rain had settled into a soft blanket of falling drops when the lid opened completely.

He searched inside, waiting for his eyes to discern who was inside, waiting for someone to scramble out, to say something.

What he saw and what he could understand didn't align.

He stared down in horror and repulsion, frozen in time and thought. In the coffin lay a decaying body, half-corpse, half-skeleton, swaddled in rotten, sunken flesh and rags. Features of what had been its face and body remained, bathed in a pool of oozing liquid. A gut-wrenching stench leapt at Nat and he turned his face away.

He had to get away from here. But he forced himself to stay.

There had been crows, lots of them.

A sheer cliff edge, a stone's throw from his parents' resting place.

Catching sight of his hands, he noticed that they were shaking, the cigarette vibrating between two yellowed fingers. He finished it. A final, quick cloud of smoke dissolved into the air. Nat stood up.

He ran his hand slowly through wavy, uncombed hair as if preparing for an important interview or a date. Took off his coat. Walked right up to the edge.

The toes of his feet were over the side.

The air clean and good. He inhaled two greedy lungfuls, then coughed.

He felt awakened again, and rejuvenated, as he used to when he came to the cliffs as a boy, having taken flowers to his parents.

His head was light. He had to catch himself and stop himself from falling. He smiled mirthlessly at that. He regained his balance.

Looked down at the surf. It was a long way. Not a chance. Die as he fell or only after he hit the surface of the sea? Or drown? He didn't care. An academic question.

Mary was in his head, a woman he had loved. He saw her face, luminous white, like a saint, teasing smile, eyes like the sea, this water.

With a conscious effort he drove the picture of her away. Otherwise he would weaken.

Was there some last idea he should hold onto? Was there a special word that would take him safely on his way.

He thought of his grandmother. She would miss him. But as she had reassured him, there was always an exit.

Up high in the left corner of the sky, the sun had emerged from cover. A big ball of fire blazing down on his face. It was beautiful. It was too late. Good fucking riddance to the world and its abundant evils.

He looked down again. The sea was unusually smooth, a gently buoyant sheet of flat, greenish silk. ...So it had all led to this.

People he had known would pass their judgements when he was gone.

"It was probably because of his parents and what happened to them," a colleague would reflect.

"He always had a rather melancholy bent," an old school friend would recount.

He surveyed the gaping sea everywhere in front of him.

They would judge him, and judge him wrongly. But it didn't matter. He would be gone. Everything would be gone forever.

The thought brought a serene smile to his lips.

"And if I'm a ghost, I'll certainly come back to haunt you all." He grinned bitterly.

Something had caught his attention.

He wanted to bury his face in his hands but he made himself look closely. The torn rags didn't reveal anything, permeated with decomposition. The rotting carcass held no clues. Only a pendant whispered its secret, its crow crying out the identity of the person who lay there. Like a Roman trinket buried with its owner to accompany him into the next life, the silver bird lay in the sunken chest of its master. Its cord was frayed but the metal had lasted, intact.

Nat sank to his knees, one hand clutching at his neck, trying to find the pendant that hung around his own neck, his mind desperately searching for explanations that didn't ring true. He was gasping, looking at what he could now recognize, with logic. Was it really his own corpse?

He wasn't dead. He knew that much for sure. He might have gone completely out of his mind. But he was alive. He wasn't dreaming and he wasn't dead.

But he couldn't think who he was, even. He wasn't sure where was. He couldn't remember how he had got there.

He took another slow, full lungful of air and released it slowly. Then he looked into the empty sky ahead of him, a haze of pale blue and cloudy white.

There was a long, spiteful squawk behind him.

He hesitated.

Another came: a harsh, unpleasant cry.

Reluctantly, he turned around.

A startling sight filled his vision. In the unkempt field of long grass and mud there stood a carpet of crows. He had never seen so many crows in one place. One flew low across the ground towards him and came to an abrupt halt, skipping comically as it went from flight into a walk and stopped. It squawked.

They hadn't been there before. Had they? He would surely have noticed. There must have been a hundred of them.

The elegant feathers of the nearest one to him called to mind Mary's shiny, black hair. He remembered her long, flowing skirts. Some of the crows hopped awkwardly around the field. Others stood perfectly still, occasionally turning their heads abruptly, seeming to ruminate.

Nat turned unsteadily and looked down at the inviting, all-enveloping waters again. On the other side, the blanket of black was edging closer to him. One menacing mass, pressing him to go ahead, hurrying him:

"Go on, do it. You're a useless waste of time."

He stood his ground. It was only a coincidence that they should be here. He needn't be intimated by them.

Again, the small birds seemed to move as one entity, pushing him over the edge.

"No," he cried.

He remained there for a few seconds, his eyes closed, relishing the unworldly sensation, one foot in heavenly dwellings. But he knew that it was over. He wouldn't do it. He didn't want to do it. He took a step back onto safe ground.

Because these birds seemed to be pushing him towards it? Because he'd thought of Mary, of hope? He didn't know the answer but he did know that there were better ways to fight suffering? There were other ways to escape from mental prisons.

Watching his every move, the birds took a collective step backwards in retreat, cautious cowards. One or two lifted off and circled, with wide, majestic wings – a grand spectacle.

He took out another cigarette. One last moment, he thought, before the long and tiring trek back to civilization, back to reality, back to all of the joy and sorrow of everyday life.

He turned to face the congregation of crows. Perhaps they hadn't goaded him towards the edge. Perhaps they had sympathized and beckoned him to safety.

...Or even, they had simply been indifferent, more concerned with their own crow lives.

Rain fell again, softly, a cleansing rain now. It pattered on the leaves on the floor, collecting in little pools where the ground wasn't even. It echoed amongst the trees, sealing off the little cemetery like a cocoon.

Like the rain, the force of Nat's terror had waned, replaced with bewildered acceptance.

He reached his hand into the steel casket, down towards the remains. He grasped the pendant. He examined it closely. There was no doubt about it. He walked through wet grass, grasping at his feet as though to suck him down into their fingers, and went up to a tree with bony branches. Carefully, he slid the worn cord over the branch, and left its medallion hanging: its silver crow eternally in mid-flight, almost seeming to fall, its wings broken, shrieking, unheard, against its will, unready to go beyond, shrieking again, bird scream…

But screaming was worse.

Nat looked upwards, into the darkness of the towering sentinel trees; they looked haughtily down at his meagre fate. It was quiet now. Nothing stirred apart from the silky veil of falling rain.

The morning light had brushed away the last specks of night. He gazed into the empty green and blue space where the coffin had lain, his tormentor, the inanimate ghost.

Then he crossed the space where it had been, leaving the small graves in the clearing behind him, leaving the past behind him, and continued on into the sea of trees, deciding to see what was there: new beginnings and unexpected adventures. And soon he was enveloped in the dark shadows, gone from sight, as though he had been an apparition, as though this life was but a dream. Or a nightmare.

Finding the Plot

Ten o' clock: Church at Night

Seya Ward, Yokohama

I leave the possible ghosts of the temple behind, hanging in their eerie, dark gloom.

So much for the temple at night. No story there.

And although I'm not enthralled with the prospect of a night-time trip to the church, I feel driven by the hands of time and the symmetry of the clock face. Once again, I feel vague, dreamy, unable to focus. But I stick to my plan and head through the dark night in the direction of the church.

When I get there, I stop in front of it, feeling conspicuous amongst the modern, suburban houses. I imagine that people are looking out of their windows at me, wondering who I am and what I'm doing there.

The church itself is suburban and modern, squeezed in between the homes. It's three stories high, with a little iron staircase to one side and plastic doors. It's not the Sagrada Familia, that's for sure. High above the door, the large cross is thin and fluorescent white, glowing chillingly in the peaceful night.

The church has plastic shutters, like house shutters, which are closed. Somebody may be inside but there it is all locked up, closed to visitors, whoever they are: worshippers, storytellers or even ghosts.

A car roars around the corner and hurtles past, forcing me to the edge of the narrow back-street. I swear at the driver, but know he won't hear it. Nearby, I notice a group of tall vending machines, three of them with their backs to the main road, forming a narrow enclave, invisible from the street. A hot green tea in a can wouldn't go amiss and I cross over to them.

I have to go around them, into a secret space behind, but these machines don't sell tea, coffee or beer. Inside are pornographic magazines, videos and even sex aids. I see a box with a picture of a doll. I laugh as it occurs to me that these machines are open all day and all night, selling their wares, just like the convenience stores, whilst I'm not allowed inside a church at this hour.

I go back to the church and crunch along the gravel path around it, alerting a suspicious light which comes on automatically to warn people about me. I continue a little further, until I'm in the centre of the car park at its rear.

I wait and hope the light will go off again. It does.

Beyond the car park, the forest and surrounding houses slope away into remote countryside. It looks more appealing than the bland building I am standing next to. Amongst the dark mystery of the trees at night, what ghosts live out their unresolved fates? ...Like me, I suppose, wandering here and there living out mine.

I give up on churches once and for all. I look over again at the silhouettes of treetops on the horizon. From where they are, the church must be invisible, just a speck in the suburbs.

Seeing Ghosts

She ran a hand down the warm spine of the dog.

Dozing, drifting off only to stop herself, but why? Dick wouldn't be coming in from the garden, or the living room where he'd been reading the paper, black-rimmed specs and a studious expression of concern on his drawn face, the anxiety of the news today.

Ah, but she also pictured him coming in with all his youth still about him. Eyes darting around the kitchen expectantly.

No use recalling the worn and helpless spectre in a hospital bed – no, don't think about that.

"I do miss him, Connie," she told the Border Collie, who frowned uncertainly. Knew something wasn't right. Disconcerted into these flights of panic that resulted in her sitting, oversized, on Ruth's lap.

Outside the window, the sky was blue. Winter falling once again. Course if Dick were here, the croquet set would be coming out for its first airing of the year. John'd be round, grandfather and grandson shouting good-humoured accusations of cheating at each other. Or back, back, earlier times, there'd be tennis or a long walk with Connie yelping and circling the fields, always coming back to them, dashing off in mad happy circles again, returning.

"Wish Dick'd return, Connie. Wish he'd come back." She waited as a tear reached her chin, then fell from the edge into nothingness. "Oh, what nonsense. Old fool, I am." Tears numbed the memories, though the empty, empty feeling lived on in the pit of her stomach, so much space in her lungs it felt like. The sun laughed at other people's jokes in the garden sky.

Ruth's eyes closed and she rested. It wasn't all that comfortable on the hard wooden chair in the study, and nobody studied anything in here any more; she'd wandered in and forgotten why, that was all. But there she rested.

It was Connie that woke her up, springing down from

her lap to stand on edge, head cocked on one side as she watched the ceiling.

Ruth followed the dog's raptured gaze upwards to the ceiling. Connie was panting excitedly now, rather like she had when she heard Dick's footsteps approaching up the garden path, home from work.

Just a high ceiling up there. Something floating – wispy, fragile. A loose strand of cobweb. Nothing but a sign that she had neglected household chores.

"What are you looking at, you silly thing?" But still Connie eyed the space above their heads anxiously, as though she'd found something.

Ruth searched the air too.

It was as she turned back to look down at the dog poised awkwardly at her feet that she saw something from the corner of her eye, a shape at the edge of her vision that oughtn't to have been there.

Standing in the doorway.

Thought she'd seen something – someone – there.

Her heart missed two beats then started clanging to compensate.

She stared.

An empty doorway. Nothing.

Well, she'd always had a good imagination, hadn't she?

Ruth walked carefully through to the living room, Connie waddling alongside and looking up at her the whole time as if Ruth would any moment open a secret door and out would step Dick, smiling and caressing and making a fuss of his dog. But Ruth didn't open the door. Not this time.

She sat down and turned on the television, recognising an old film she had seen many times and that was halfway through. It was when the ads came on and she'd got to her feet to make a pot of tea that the photograph clattered over.

It slid in slow motion from its place on the mantelpiece and fell to the tiles of the electric fireplace where it landed with a crash and lay there, a crack tracing its way from the top of the glass surface to the bottom.

It was surely a sign – from spiteful fate itself; it was their wedding photo that had fallen from grace.

Ruth kept very still.

She glanced at the space left by the picture on the mantelpiece. Odd that it should fall like that. She searched the big green room around her.

She could imagine that he was there with her.

The smell of Dick's cologne was here. The old, ever-present tang of citrus and soft wood. Still lingering on from his when he was alive?

She stood stock still for ten minutes, waiting for another sign. Connie slept, curled up in Dick's armchair. Her shiny black fur coat rose and fell as she breathed. A slight wheezing noise audible in the stillness.

Then Ruth shook her head vigorously, walked over to where the photo lay in its shattered frame and picked it up. She examined her young self and Dick on their wedding day, Christmas Day – now separated in the picture by a dark, uneven crack – and friends and relatives gathered behind, most of them gone now.

It had fallen because of the noise of the television. Vibrations, that was why. …There were no ghosts.

In the kitchen, she made tea and took it to the living room, along with the big red tin of biscuits.

"No-one to tell me not to!" she told the dog. "And don't you go whispering to anyone if I polish off the whole box." She dropped one on the carpet for him.

Her face was sad. She would have liked Dick to frown at her when she helped herself to a third Bourbon biscuit.

Ruth didn't want to watch any more of the film, and fetched her coat from the closet instead.

"Come on if you're coming," she called and Connie appeared, looking a little surprised at the idea of a walk at this time of day but pleased at the good turn of luck.

She was unaware of Connie at the end of the lead, almost did see ghosts in the street – memories, in fact, of walking this way every day arm in arm with Dick, religiously posting his Pools coupon in the red box at the end of the road, setting out on a long journey early in the morning at the beginning of a holiday, stopping to talk to neighbours in the Summer. There seemed to be something missing from the road, as though a building had disappeared or a tree been cut down. But nothing visible had altered.

The sea came into view, soothing green water on the horizon. The smell of salt made her young again. She might have been eighteen not eighty, with a life ahead of her.

The wind rose up, seagulls brushed from side to side on its currents, slipping and sliding helplessly in the air. Connie waited patiently, watching the birds in the sky and the waves rippling in.

There was no-one on the beach. Great big openness surrounded her. Rare cars on the road up behind her were all that disturbed the tranquillity from time to time.

Blowing and trembling around her head, the wind flapped her scarf up in front of her face.

It was easy to let herself believe there was something strange about today. It had been exactly a year, after all.

Ruth eyed the hilltop away to the right. She could see the trees up there shaking more violently in the wind and felt drawn.

She made her way to the foot of the slope, grasped the metal handrail and step by step made her way to the top, the dog monitoring her progress. Then she joined Connie, who had already taken her place of old in front of the bench, and sat down.

Blackness had descended. Orange lights further down the coast were blocked out by the curtain of restless trees encircling her. But she refused to feel afraid. This was her spot now, just as it had belonged to Dick and her.

She was all alone but it didn't feel that way up here. She didn't feel cold, even this late in the day. Could almost feel Dick right here, or his ghost watching over her, just behind the bench. Her thoughts glided over the past, words entered her mind, contextless things Dick had said to her and she to him. The rustling of the dark bushes in front mingled with the words she heard in her head and the waves breaking below on the beach.

She remained still, listening to the sounds of the dark.

Could almost feel his hand resting on her shoulders now...

Almost... but not quite.

Feats of imagination, that was the best she could get.

"Connie, I wish there were ghosts, I do you know."

Connie looked up at her understandingly.

"Oh, I used to be ever so frightened of such things, I was an awful coward, but what I'd give to see ghosts now." She stroked the soft fur on Connie's back. "What I'd give to see one now."

She got to her feet, and cautiously descended the precipitous steps.

There were no ghosts. Only faint memories, paler than ghosts. Was his face exactly as she remembered, growing dimmer in her mind with every day? Even their wedding photograph was broken.

It was when she was least expecting it that Dick came to her at last.

She was kneeling before the fireplace, holding the broken wedding photograph and looking forlornly at the picture of the past. The lights in the living room were dim.

Connie was somewhere far away, asleep at this time of night.

She had forgotten what time it was, forgotten all about time. Traced the outline of Dick's face with her fingertip, fingers of lead and heart like lead, so heavy.

She looked at the young woman – beautiful, slim girl with waves of deep brown hair – there was no denying her beautiful big eyes.

Dick with hair swept back, black and clean, and clear eyes staring out, a little unsure, a little wistful.

He touched her shoulder and she turned to look up at him.

They spoke no words, just looked into one another's faces.

Joyful tears welled in her eyes. "Oh, Dick."

He didn't speak, just smiled that melancholy smile.

"You came back."

They held each other for a thousand hours.

The sun crept into her room in the morning, waking her

gently. She lay there, recalling the visions of the night.

Connie knew Ruth had woken up and stood on hind legs, resting front paws on the bed and licking the outstretched hand. Ruth stroked her head.

She whispered sleepily to the dog, "Oh there are ghosts all right. There is such a thing." And turned away from the window. To sleep some more, and perhaps see ghosts again.

Finding the Plot

Eleven o' clock: Forest at Night

Seya Ward, Yokohama

On the brief walk to the forest, the adrenalin is buzzing around my body. I can't help but think about all the discomforting scenes I've ever stumbled across in films. I picture blood on walls, witches dancing at the bottom of a garden – then I snap out of it.

But the quietness in the dirt street as I move along between the sleepy houses, the freezing, dark air, my recent dead ends, and the fact that I'm now intending to go into the middle of a forest, all alone and at night – all these things lend a sense of foreboding. I do my best to dispel grim ideas. But it's almost as if I'm trying to think sinister thoughts just to terrify myself, trying to remember something.

I focus on real things. Passing the witch-like little tree I noticed on my last outing to the woods, I instinctively look over my shoulder. I'm soon approaching the towering spikes of trees I had seen from the suburbs.

The icy mud cracks noisily under my boots. It crosses my mind that the residents of the few houses I have passed at the outskirts of the forest might be alarmed if they spot a stranger in a woolly hat and burly, dark coat and boots tramping off into the trees. I stop at the edge and gaze back towards the houses. A silhouette moves against the light of a bedroom, then blocks out the world by slicing a curtain across the window in one short, sharp action. Hands deep in my pockets, I turn around again and scrutinize the gentle hill leading into the darkness. I hadn't realised that it would be quite so dark. If I look straight up, I can see the shapes of the highest leaves against quite a bright, brownish sky, but directly ahead there is nothing but intense black. I proceed ten more metres, and pause again. Look back once more. A few more trees behind me now, the same houses, nobody near, nobody following me. I search the woods at my sides, checking for crazed psychopaths or degenerate perverts. Nothing stirs in here, although looking directly upwards, each tree is gently stirring with small, circular movements in a breeze. The top of one tree is broken and hangs by a precarious thread high above me.

I think, once again, of what my ex-fiancée would say:

"Writers and artists end up killing themselves and going crazy. They're always mad."

I'd laugh, and argue that while some might be mad to start with, writing didn't have to turn you that way. And she would remain skeptical.

Now I find myself wondering if there was something in the things that she said. I wonder if there are other writers here in the inky blackness amongst the trees, searching for their own stories …wandering ghosts like me …or simply a snapping, falling branch, dangerous enough.

I refuse to abandon the search before the cycle is complete. Having made it unscathed through the darkness this far, I must absorb the frigid atmosphere, hunting the forest for signs of inspiration. I survey the surrounding silhouettes of trees, like weeds in a giant's pond; they intertwine and, looking down at me, make me feel like a fish at the bottom of some cold, watery depths.

I spy a severed head amongst the leaves. I scold myself and shake off the imagining. An aural hallucination: the voices of small children, a boy and a girl, play-fighting nearby. He is mocking her. It is just the conjuring of other, natural sounds into what my subconscious fears most …I think.

All the sounds of dogs and birds and cheerful, bright colours and people have gone. I wonder where the crows have gone. I feel haunted by time, by reality.

I suppose that there is a tranquil beauty here. I try to breathe it in.

Continuing along the path, I'm feel as though I'm drawing nearer and nearer the frightening ocean bottom of the forest. This really is the realm of spirits. I remember an ink painting I saw in an exhibition at the town hall in Ofuna. It stole my attention. I had to sit on the little bench for viewers and look at it, hypnotized:

With a background of white flowers, a woman in kimono presides over a small, blazing fire amongst the trees in a forest at night. In the flames, dance the embers of a stack of letters that she feeds to it, watching as they turn to ash. Her face is nothing more than a white, blank mask, in contrast to the black night all around her.

The sad story of a woman and her ill-fated love affair, perhaps, or something more profound.

The painting was five canvases wide, displayed in a little gallery where only the creations of young, unknown artists were shown. The central canvas consisted only of pure black night, and it seemed somehow fitting that this absence of anything should have been in the centre of the whole creation.

I can no longer see a single thing. I am walking through a void, with the foolishness of a voluntary blind man.

I continue as far as I can but it's hopeless and, finally, I turn around and trace my way back, no thread of wool to follow, no trail of breadcrumbs, just foolish hope and survival instinct. I find myself on a frozen footpath, icy mud occasionally squelching loudly beneath me. I slow my pace, and tread cautiously, hearing the silence. Sometimes a creak or groan from the gusty wind permeates the stillness. I look behind me to make sure I'm alone. Of course I am alone. What other fool would have come here?

I'm careful to avoid overhanging branches and twigs, though my smooth progress is largely owing to fortune.

The shapes of houses come into sight, brown halos around their roofs. Feeling a surge of relief, I look back. I commend myself on my bravery and reprimand myself for my foolishness. And though I have survived, still no story has presented itself and there is no resolution.

Carbon Copy

I shivered as I sat on the lumpy mattress in the bedsit, a clichéd artist in the lurid colours of German expressionist painters. I surveyed the walls, the colour of badly cared for teeth.

I looked at the clock. Four o'clock.

It was always four o'clock, for some reason.

The ceiling shook with the tremors of the bed upstairs, occasional moans of joy like the sound of an animal being repeatedly stabbed, seeping through the floor above and into my life, animals moaning in pointed stabs of sound, emphasising my aloneness and my failures. Four o'clock in the afternoon, for God's sake. Didn't they have any hobbies? Perhaps that was their hobby.

I hadn't always lived in such a lustreless environment. Not far from here, I had been happy. I remembered my student days, cavorting in green ocean parks, swimming through blue skies of laughter and potential, hopefully knocking tennis balls back over the net to Mick, my grinning, sardonic cat of a friend, smart and awkward, athletic and often drunken. I was the idealist. You could make a living from painting, I claimed. There was such a thing as a perfect love, I argued, or at least, one true love.

There was also the memory of drinking in the student bar with Pavel, who told me I needed to finish what I started, for once.

"Fuck you," I told him, but I suspect that he…

I looked at the rice paper drenched in black ink and tacked to the walls of my little living space: a mountain scene displayed above the cooker, a priest making his way along a path in jagged hills decorating the space above the fridge, some sort of ghost hanging on the door, a woman in a white kimono on the cupboard, in the bough of a tall tree – all black and white and shades therein – and all over every spare space on the walls abstract shapes in all the grey colours of the morgue-rainbow: grey and grey and grey and grey, a pretty morgue-rainbow.

One painting differed from the others. This one was in a thick bamboo frame and occupied the space above my headboard and pillow. My mind glowed when I looked at that. It was what I aspired to. It was everything I wanted to achieve. I had purchased it in a small, backstreet art gallery where no-one seemed to go. I had wandered down there after a day in the office, a zombie released, on parole from the administrative tasks of Dickensian desperados.

In a moment of escapism, in the full knowledge that our bank balance was zero, I had made the impulse buy.

I would frequent the little art gallery in the back streets on my way home from the office. I think I must have fallen in love with the simple strokes of the ink paintings there. Long before, at school, I had been a very average painter. I could draw a likeness but that was about it. Once I set foot in that gallery, however, I applied myself. I was mesmerised by the haunting blacks, whites and greys of these pictures and dreamt of producing one like them of my own.

At first, I would sit for thirty minutes, then hours, then whole weekends, quickly getting used to holding the brush so far up its stem, cherishing the ideology of the ancients that once you had begun to set the strokes on the page, nothing could be changed. I liked the circular grinding of the ink stone in its tray, producing thick, black blood that would be used to daub the rice paper.

I began to improve. It became my obsession.

I continued visiting the little gallery and others, too. I would stare into the strokes of the paintings. There was meaning there amongst the recluses in caves, monks toiling up mountainsides with sacks over their backs, gowned women with hair piled high on their heads with combs.

"It's a different world, isn't it?" she said.

It was the first time she had spoken to me, the woman who tended the shop. She always stood behind the counter at the far end of the shop, absorbed in her phone.

"That's what I was just thinking," I said honestly.

She had left her usual station and come over to stand next to me. Her hair was straight and bobbed. Her face was shy and pale. It was kind and humorous. She was on the thin side, like a malnourished ghost.

"Have you been to Asia?" she said.

"No. But I'm buying lottery tickets," I said.

She chuckled.

I regretted my words. People who came to shops like these weren't lottery hopers. They had made their money and were here to drop some of it. They were out to add to their collections or impress their friends. Poor artists didn't buy originals by other artists.

"Well, don't choose number 4!" she said.

"Number 4? Why not?"

"Unlucky number," she said, smiling conspiratorially.

"It is?"

"Yes. In Asian culture."

"That's a shame," I said, pointing at the picture of a black square. "That's the one I like." It had a number 4 and its title on a little plaque with some information about the artist.

"Do you really?" she said with surprise.

"It's like looking right into space," I said. "It's very calming."

"Well, fair enough," she said. "I'm not going to tell you not to buy it. I'd lose my job."

I smiled.

"Is this your shop?"

"It's my Dad's. He paints."

"Did he paint anything here?"

"Yes. Over there."

She pointed to a painting on the other side of the gallery, five panels that made up one image: a white figure of a woman, standing amongst trees and flowers, feeding pieces of paper solemnly into a fire. I'd observed it many times.

"I love that picture," I said.

"You do? I'll pass on your feedback," she chuckled.

"It's unbelievable how so much colour is conjured up just with a black ink stick. And it's very atmospheric and moody."

She nodded. "He's very good. But you know what? He was accused of stealing the idea for it."

"From who?"

"Another painter who lived long ago."

"And did he?"

"Not deliberately. There are some similarities – but you know what they say, *Everything has already been said*."

"Including that," I joked.

She laughed.

"Do you paint?" I asked, enjoying looking into her black eyes as we chatted.

"I try."

She must be an amateur like me, I thought.

"That's mine," she laughed. "Number 4."

"Oh!"

Perhaps that was really the start of everything.

Soon after, I bought the painting of the black square.

And I rolled up my sleeves and painted more furiously. Perhaps I should have spent less time doing that and more on advancing my career, but I wasn't interested in that. I began painting more ethereal, ghostly apparitions on the sheets of rice paper.

The only thing that troubled me was that I didn't seem able to come up with anything very original. Every stroke was an echo of others that had gone before. Perhaps like she had told me, everything had already been said.

Buying the picture had been the final straw. Catherine finally threw out her useless, hopeless husband, as she called me. Perhaps my subconscious had wanted exactly that. She told me that I should have spent more time advancing my career and less time painting.

"You don't even use any colour," she said, exasperated.

I don't think the cost alone would have enraged her so much. Yes, we didn't have such sums to spare. If we had, we would have been moving house, or having the floorboards in the attic reinforced, or the walls of the house repointed, or the damp treated, or the banister repaired.

We could have taken a holiday in the sun. Mexico had been our dream. Spain would have sufficed.

We could have breathed more easily – at least for a little while, these humans dreaming of beautiful lives free of bills, inflation and speeding tickets.

It was the painting she didn't like. To say it wasn't her cup of tea would be an understatement. The fact that it was nothing but sweeping black strokes, a black mass with no discernible subject... that was what really pissed her off.

"It's just a black square! How could you? You're out of your mind!"

She stared at me with an uncomprehending expression. She didn't know words that could verbalise the disdain she felt in that moment. She was going out of her own mind with rage. She was red in the face with a brilliance I would never use in my monochrome artwork, my black and white world.

I knew that it seemed strange to have spent so much on such a minimal image. But there was something about it... and something about owning it... that promised an epiphany for me. Perhaps I had cracked, one bird escaping from the aviary in my mind. I didn't think so.

And my wife, who spent our money on potions and lotions that she had read on the internet would bring us joy... she wasn't blameless in the whole equation.

My reveries were interrupted by a faint tapping on the door of my bedsit.

It was such a feeble rapping that I almost ignored it all together; yet that almost inaudible sound announced some shit that was going to upend my life as I'd known it. And as though my heart knew what misgivings it should have, that soft scratching cooked up a feeling of angst in my lungs; a pendulum swung across the pit of my belly.

Perhaps I would have done well to ignore it.

An old lady stood on the other side of the threshold. Her hair had a purple tint. Her face was full of echoes and her mouth was judgmental.

I eyed her judgmentally.

Her lips bared into a beaming smile. "Mr Streamfall?"

"Correct."

"Magnificent."

She took an envelope (purple of course) from her handbag (yellowy-brown like the sickly walls of my bedsit) and handed it to me.

"If this is an eviction, I'm not accepting this document," I said. "I know my rights."

Wasn't that the mantra of all the fucked-over victims of the ravaging system, all poor fuckers who have no chance of their rights ever meaning a damned thing?

"Oh!" She clapped her hands together like a child getting a Halloween treat. "You're the winner!"

"Oh, a sales trick. Door to door?"

I respected her endeavour.

"No, no, Mr Streamfall," she corrected me. "The competition. I'm from the Debonair Art Society. Your entry won first prize."

I hesitated. This didn't seem in the script.

"Are you sure?" I said, baffled.

"Now don't be modest. I know that you probably didn't expect to win anything. That's very humble and very becoming. Now, the cash prize will be presented at the Winners' Reception, which will also be the vernissage for the paintings on display."

She produced a form and studied it.

"Will your work be for sale?" she said, perusing the words on her piece of paper.

I stared at her.

This all sounded like a mistake. I had entered a competition that I'd seen advertised, in a moment of rare optimism and self-belief, but what I had chosen to submit didn't seem to me to be anything particularly out of the ordinary.

"Are you willing to sell it if a viewer wants to buy it? Or is it for your private collection."

Even as I laughed at this, for the first time, I beheld the outstretched hand of redemption.

For her part, she seemed to register the shitty living space behind me. A brief look of confusion brushed over her face. But her eyes shrugged and she returned to the matter at hand.

A small voice at the back of my head wanted to lie and tell her that I hadn't entered her competition, that I wasn't John Streamfall, that this was a mistake. A strange little part of me wanted just to be unknown, to wallow in my failure, my anonymity, here in the most functional of spaces, with no-one to have to account to. The prospect of success was frightening. I didn't feel ready for recognition.

But another part of me craved validation – not to mention the prize.

As though she were telepathic, she announced, "First prize is a motorcaravan!"

She looked so happy. I frowned. That was a kick in the nuts.

"I don't drive. You know, living in London and everything…"

"Sell it! They're ever so valuable."

I could, I supposed. I decided to go along with the whole charade, pretend I could be a winner, act as though I knew what I was doing.

"Now, sign here." She thrust a crumpled, damp page in front of me along with a pink fountain pen.

I scrawled my name.

"Wonderful."

"When is the viewing?"

"In four weeks' time. You'll receive a letter with details of dress code, the schedule and so on."

"Dress code?" I snuck a furtive glance at my wardrobe.

"Yes, tuxedo and black tie, Mr Streamfall!" she grinned, rather manically.

And then she was gone in a flurry of goodbyes and congratulations and it really was a wonderful painting, she said.

I suppose it was the kind of good day that Regular Joes experienced, where the joy of life had the potential to balance its suffering.

I would be able to move out of the bedsit I inhabited like some nineteenth century Russian literary character and perhaps even live in the studio flat at the top of the Victorian building, It would be a literal and metaphorical promotion.

Had things stayed as they were, it would have been a good day, one that I would have remembered and talked about to my future art students and grandchildren as the start of my vindicated life. …If things had stayed as they were. But something about the script I'd been given in life, or some flaw in my karma, would prevent things from unfolding so simply…

The woman looked exactly like she had before – but there was something very different about her. I couldn't quite put my finger on it, at first. Was it the expression on her lips? They looked more tightly pursed. He hair was tinted orange this time – but why wouldn't a woman change her hair colour from tinted purple to tinted orange? Her eyes seemed a little smaller, birdlike, more penetrating. Maybe she was having a bad day.

"Mr Screamfall'?"

"Streamfall," I corrected her.

It was a strange opening in any case. She knew very well who I was from the last time. It wasn't as though there could be very many of us hiding in my cramped bedsit.

Dementia? Senility?

I presumed that she had come bearing administrative tidings. It had only been a week since her last visit and it wasn't time for the exhibition yet. That was three weeks away.

"It seems that there has been a mix-up."

That stopped me in my tracks.

Here it was, I thought, like the end of a nice dream, like waking up with all of the same problems you'd forgotten about.

It had a reassuring familiarity, however. It had the beauty of perfect symmetry.

"I didn't win?" I stated. It explained her changed countenance.

I peered at her. She seemed to be clenching her teeth very hard. Her face seemed in the shade of a cloud. Her shoulders trembled. Was she about to cry?

"No, that's right. You didn't win," she hissed.

I nodded. The dreams of selling a motorcaravan and how I would spend the cash evaporated.

She stepped into my flat.

"Hey."

"You!" she said, pointing a withered finger at me. It was bonier and more withered than her predecessor's. "You should be ashamed of what you did."

I backed away from her, further into the room.

"Charlatan!" she continued, on a roll now. "If you can't conceive of anything original of your own, then don't paint at all! Shame on you for copying someone else's work and palming it off as your own!"

"I don't know what you're talking about," I said.

Even as I said it, I sensed that something was amiss. It was true that I had felt differently about the paintings I had created after buying that black square, hanging there on my wall, out of place with the dirty dishes in the sink and the ancient cooker. Before, my paintings had been a little staid, I now thought, as though they weren't really from me at all. Since acquiring the black square from the gallery and hanging it in my small room, not only had I begun having the weirdest dreams, but also I was painting freely, ravenously, like a swooping raven, sometimes painting a swooping raven, and the subjects were more striking, I thought.

And hadn't my theory been correct? I'd won a prize.

Now it had been taken away from me and I stood accused of stealing someone else's ideas. Like a character in a Kafka novel, I had done nothing but here I was, on trial. The difference was I knew the crime I was supposed to have committed.

I gazed over at the black square on the wall. I wondered about the painting I was supposed to have copied. It wasn't possible to have come up with a painting exactly the same as someone else's when you looked at how specific my work was. And I had based it on a dream that I had had. There was no way that some other painter, previous to me, had had the exact same dream, then created the exact same vision.

"There will be no motorcaravan," she sniffed, "and your painting" – she spat the word – will be returned to you forthwith." She turned on her heels and marched back out.

A burning sense of injustice boiled my blood. I knew that I could fight this. But for some reason, I smiled. I no longer cared, I decided.

A few days later, I was having a cup of coffee with Gen, the gallery assistant and painter of black squares, in the *Missing Bean* café, not far from the little gallery. I had told her the story of what had happened.

"That's unbelievable," she said, gazing at me with those spacious black eyes. "What was your painting of?"

"That's the thing," I explained. "It was made up of four sheets of paper – a little like your father's one in the gallery."

"Copycat," she teased. "What was on each one?"

"It was a little dreamy, really. There was a figure – a man – walking in different locations, searching for something. In the first one, he was in a forest, in the second he was standing outside a church, the next he was at a temple on a hill, and then in the final one he was fading slightly from sight. There were crows flying about in the sky."

"Sounds great! Who is he?"

"I think he's a ghost, searching for something. Every hour, he visits the places he used to know, wandering, feeling like something's not right, like he doesn't quite belong – but not knowing why …and repeating it all every day, hour by hour, locked in a cycle."

She nodded. "What's he looking for?"

"The story of what happened to him. He can't let it go."

"Very good," she said, pretending to clap. "But you know what you did wrong?"

"Tell me."

"Four parts," she grinned. "I told you: four is unlucky."

I laughed.

"I didn't even think it was that good. I was surprised when the first woman said I'd won."

"What are you going to do?"

"Nothing."

She smiled. "Are you sure?"

"Yes," I said. I sipped the strong, black liquid in my cup. "To be honest, I feel like I'm going to stop painting. Don't get me wrong. I love all that Chinese ink. It's breathtaking. But I feel like I've done what I wanted to do – whether I won anything or not."

"Okay," she nodded.

"Anyway," I said. "Perhaps it *is* time I spent more time on my career."

She reached across the table and touched my hand with a delicate finger. "That's fair enough. As long as you're sure. It does seem very unfair."

"I am sure," I said.

I took her hand in mine. It was warm and, somehow, reassuringly familiar.

Finding the Plot

Midnight: Chasing Shadows

Seya Ward, Yokohama / A Void

Walking away from the forest, I shudder. What a ridiculous existence. Do I have to walk around all of these places for ever more? It's not working. This is futile, going on and on in search of something that probably doesn't even exist, repeating the same cycle, over and over, finding nothing to drive my story onwards.

I smile to myself. Perhaps I should write a haiku instead. It's short and simple. No need for a plot or characters.

What a fool, walking around cities and forests, night and day, putting myself in the way of danger and exhaustion. It is turning into a nightmare. I've become so occupied with looking for something that I've forgotten what it was that was missing, why it was that I set out upon this quest.

I reach the cold, quiet road and listen to my boots striding with certainty on the gravel and mud, and I realise that I've lost the original thought that set me on this quest. The only thing that all these setting share in common – temples, churches, forests, night, day, people, no people – is that they reinforce my feeling of utter isolation.

I clank up the iron steps to my house, go in and switch on the television. The news informs me of the stabbing and death of a twenty-six year old teacher – the same age as me, even looks like me   who scolded a thirteen year old boy for being late. Later he explained that he hadn't intend to do it, but when the teacher showed him no fear, he became angry and killed her.

I feel like I've seen that news before. I can't quite remember. I suppose all news recycles and copies itself.

I think I'll sit here for a long while, revelling in the absence of all excitement. It's hard enough trying to sort through the confusion in my own head. It seems continually to project onto every scene that I see, every place I go and everyone I talk to. It's hard to think clearly.

The news story continues. Relatives cry and talk about justice.

We spend our lives looking for the answer and then we're suddenly dead. I spend my time looking for a story, and now it's over.

I feel myself disappearing again, spiralling into a whirlpool of lost time.

Molly (Revisited)

Molly was practising an etude, a sandwich waiting to be eaten at her convenience. The cello, she often told me, is a salubrious thing. And I could see bubbles of well-being sailing about her, dancing to the long draws of the bow. This was her new life, well-chosen.

Finding the Plot

Midday: The Search

Seya Ward, Yokohama

The air is glassy, pale blue, but all isn't still, for the yellow-green dresses of the trees sway majestically, bending all the way over, all the leaves shimmering and rustling in the sunlight.

The snow is evaporating, leaving patches of brown earth to breathe freely once again after their cold suffocation. The houses gleam dryly, having survived one more trial. In between two houses, drivers navigate their metal boxes, back to normal speed after the snow, in and out of my sight for an instant.

I look across the valley of rubble, mud and thawing whiteness, where men have come to put up ladders and drape pieces of blue plastic and manoeuvre hungry, churning machines, week in and week out, for over a year – mysteriously without actually constructing anything yet.

My eyes focus on the two-storied red brick house with a brown, tiled roof where some large, black birds circle and shriek with certainty. They bounce down onto the tiles, but only for a moment before they launch away into the air again. Crows don't flutter; they glide. They make long arcs as, wings outstretched like a crucifixion, they sweep around and through the telegraph wires. With elbows propped on my low table, I rest pursed lips against joined hands, considering the birds at length.

They seem content. They're doing what they do best. What they were made to do? But not me. I put the cap on the fountain pen and lay it down. There is a blank page open beneath it. I need to find a story, a worthy plot to write. I will go in search of it.

With newfound resolution, I get to my feet and fetch my thick coat and hat. I go out and close the door firmly behind me, breathing in the cold air. My mind is like a crowd of gigantic, veering, howling crows, falling sideways through the clear, blue, icy sky.

Epiphany

The crash was unavoidable with my mind so far away. Miles away. Turning over and over the ins and outs of my final savage clash with Sara. I had leapt at the opportunity of transfer to a remote part of the country. There was to be no going back.

Until the crash. As soon as it happened, an unhailed change came over me. I didn't try to explain it although it was odd that it seized my thoughts while I was still heaving the car door open and staggering from the wreckage. I concluded, even in the midst of the sickly silence following the collision, that all my reasoning until then had somehow been misguided.

The dirt street was deserted but for the shells of our two defeated steel monsters which had come to a premature end of their lifespan, beyond hope of restoration.

The other driver's head had thumped violently to a rest on his steering wheel. I gaped through rising smoke and steam, and his shattered windscreen, at the somnolent figure.

Anguish squeezed my heart in an iron grip, the blood draining away and leaving an empty sensation of disbelief. But I knew that I could do nothing for him.

I wondered how I had escaped so lightly, although it flashed through my mind that it was justice that I had survived and not he, for the now-lifeless corpse had screamed into my car out of the nowhere of a black side street, his face ignited with a maniacal glare. God knew what had possessed him.

My phone had been thrown from its cradle and, after a brief hunt in the dirt and amongst the shattered glass in the back of the car, I found it – a lump of cracked plastic and metal, no longer fit to serve as the life support machine it had become. I needed a person and their mobile phone – not to report the accident, though I would do that too, but to call Sara. I saw that I had to reverse what I had instigated, before I lost her forever.

I checked each part of my body in turn for broken bones, cuts or lack of movement. My head felt painfully tight and I was sure that I would be sick as I could hardly contain the queasiness in my stomach. For a minute, I couldn't focus my thoughts or vision, could barely remember who I was. I felt far away, slipping out of sync with the present moment. The crystals of glass crunching under my shoes brought me back to reality. I could walk.

There was no sign of anyone, and the only telephone booth I passed had been converted into a library, books by Stephen King and Lee Child lined up on shelves in place of the handset that had once been its function, cobwebs hanging in the corners. Who stopped to pick up or drop off a book in this remote location, I couldn't imagine for the life of me.

The last lone house had vanished into the blood-red backwash of my rear lights more than ten minutes before the accident. I didn't know which way to turn, and stood beside my crushed car, panic suddenly pumping adrenalin around my body much too fast. I could hear my own heart beating.

I found myself drifting toward the trees, drawn by the smoke twisting through the black trunks. It was coiling up above the dense mass of trees on the opposite side of the road.

I strode into them, guessing that there was a house with a chimney or bonfire. In my bewilderment, it failed even to cross my mind that it was more rational to stay on the road, or that these first trees were part of a cavernous forest.

The air was damp and the way murky. Drips fell from above, wetting my hair and chilling my neck. The invisible trees that I passed tore my grey suit. But I hurried on. I splashed through muddy puddles, frantically trying to keep sight of the vague orange glimmer in the distance through the tangle of trees, and trying again to ignore the sick feeling in my stomach.

The amber blur was growing larger, whilst the darkness hemming me in seemed to become even blacker. Only now did it occur to me that I had made a mistake in my choice of direction, the jagged trees towering down unforgivingly, and small cuts appearing on my hands from the claws of my imprisoners. I had no choice but to keep going until I reached the light.

But as the small fire came into view at last, I slowed my pace and came to an apprehensive halt. I thought that I must be dreaming. Slowly it dawned on me with unwanted certainty, however, that the crash and now this were all too real.

She stood almost with her back to me, a graceful figure with unnaturally long, dark hair. With her head partially bowed, as if in great sadness, from time to time she took a piece of folded paper from a pile clutched in her left hand, and fed the insatiable flames.

I lingered in the gloom at the edge of the small clearing, unable to move, watching as she patiently continued her solemn ritual with an air of resigned tragedy. My purpose had been sucked into obscurity, as though the woman I was beholding and her dancing tongues of flame were all I had been seeking. For a few useless seconds, I tried to rouse myself but couldn't, unable to remember more than a deep black void enveloping me, in which each way I turned led to deeper nothingness. Instead, my eyes drank in her long, cobalt blue kimono, which glowed eerily in the dim light, and the gentle curves of her figure. I couldn't turn away, mesmerised by the incongruence of her appearance and the setting. Still the pieces of paper came, and I watched each one with unthinking awe, realising at length that they were envelopes.

As the silent trees began to stir above me in a momentary breeze, my senses repossessed me. I couldn't fathom the strange apparition, but likewise I had no idea where I was. I had to find a house, or a telephone.

I called out, "Excuse me."

She didn't answer, entranced by her grave ceremony.

"Excuse me," I said again, taking a nervous step forward.

Still no movement.

I walked cautiously towards her, not wanting to cause alarm, and uncertain myself of what to expect from her. I was standing right behind her when I spoke again.

"Excuse me. I need some help."

She turned abruptly, obviously startled, but in that instant my horror was the greater for she began screaming and screaming like a madwoman at me, envelopes falling as she covered her whole face except for her black eyes.

And I was terrified.

The colour of her skin was abnormally white, her features beautiful but aged before their time, a glint of distraught wisdom in her eyes, as though she knew of things she shouldn't. She recoiled towards the fire, as if it was *I* that was haunting *her*, and I too drew away, partly to get away from her, and partly for fear that she would step back into the fire. She didn't say a coherent word, only howling in contagious terror that curdled the blood in my veins.

I backed away into the veil of bony trees, and finally tore my eyes from the ethereal illumination of the clearing, the fire and the woman, breaking quickly into a run. The branches snatched at me with renewed savagery, gashing my head once, and gouged scratches on my face that the car crash had failed to.

I remembered the cars. How many traumas could I encounter?

The way ahead was a fog of black and darker black; I was a blind man, with no knowledge of what I was running into. Through the darkness I scurried, my panic threefold now with my head a spinning haze of Sara, the kimono woman and the knowledge that I was lost in an immense forest. I could stumble violently through its talons for hours without escape. I was sure that I was running in circles. I was bound to meet the woman again.

At last, unexpectedly, the trees were behind me. I was on another silent road, panting asthmatically, hot sweat coating my face. There was no sign of a house, but I closed my eyes in silent prayer at having escaped the web of the forest.

I turned away from any trees I could see. I didn't want to look back but risked one glance to get my bearings. Only an inscrutable facade of wood and leaves. I couldn't see smoke any more. I had come a long way and it was darker than before.

Having walked for fifteen minutes through the blindfolding night that hung over the track, I was beginning to despair of finding help when, at last, a small building came into view, a square silhouette shedding a yellow glow on one side. I began to jog again, and soon was standing outside a small house in a bad state of repair. I thanked God again as I saw the light seeping through curtains upstairs; someone was at home.

I didn't hesitate to thump the black, iron lion's head against the heavy door several times, shuddering as I remembered the head of the other driver on his steering wheel. I thought I could hear someone stirring within and brushed my dishevelled hair with the filthy palm of my hand, straightening my torn suit as best I could.

"Who is it?" an elderly voice called out.

"I'm sorry to disturb you. I've had a car accident and badly need to use a phone," I said urgently.

Again she called, "Who is it?"

I repeated my words more loudly. Perhaps she was a little deaf.

Finally, after what seemed an age, the door creaked open a reluctant inch. In my eagerness, I tried to push the door a little further. On the other side, I saw an old lady, in her floral dressing gown, anxious face and frail figure. A chain on the door resisted my desperation.

"I need to use your phone..." I began, but to no avail. With a dreadful sense of recognition, I was witnessing the same events as I had in the forest. Upon seeing me, she stepped back and screamed, but the scream died in her petrified throat. She could no longer get it out of her lungs, able only to stand trembling as if she had fallen into a lake of ice, her mouth open in a limp hole.

In desperation, I foolishly tried to push at the door again, which rattled stubbornly on its chain until I found, to my sickly horror, that I was inside the house. Impossibly I had passed through the door.

I gaped at the woman, unsure whether to apologise, implore or turn and run again. Before I could decide, she was clutching at her throat, her frantic eyes now fixed on mine, wide with a terrible recognition that seemed to reach beyond both of us. She was gasping and wheezing for breath that would not come to her mercy. Slowly, the struggle for breath subsided, leaving only the silence between us. Her face turned as white as a ghost, and then she was lying like an ugly rock on the floor.

And in the space that she had stood occupying, I stared ahead into a wide mirror on the wall.

I could see no reflection, nothing but the old, brown, wooden front door behind me, silent and indifferent. Desperately, I searched for myself – my face, my eyes, my hair, my outline – anything that would prove I was still there – but only the unbroken form of the door stared back.

In the distance, I heard a murder of crows caw aggressively, and then the noise receded into the distance, echoing in waves until it had faded altogether and was no more.

Epilogue: Words Unheard

I trust that my decision to publish, rather than set fire to, Keshava's writings was the right one and has brought joy to its readers. I speculate as to whether he will come across the translated and published version of his stories. My inner voice tells me, however, that he won't. I picture him in a mountain, or a forest, or seeking calm in the busiest *City by Day* or *City at Night.*

At the same time, I hope that at some point in the future the crows will bring us more of his words and whatever new realities and truths he has discovered. Once again, however, my instinct is that the crows will keep their counsel and deliver nothing further. We will of course see, in time.

I trust that Naoto 'Kehsava' Karasuma has not lost the plot. I feel sure, beyond doubt, that he has not. May you discover your own plot, and never lose it.

Translation: September 2024.

Acknowledgements

My deepest thanks to Nick Tanner for the rational eye and rational 'T', as well as the speedy and invaluable feedback, and of course for being the original pioneer. A big thank you to Bob Tsukada-Bright for his encouragement and all of the uplifting conversations, which always leave me smiling and inspired. Thank you to Nick Page for services as creative muse and (sometimes ignored) artistic curator. Heartfelt thanks to Mum, for listening to my ramblings, and for all of our chats about books and everything else. Thank you, too, John, for the first Word Processor.

And finally, a deep bow of thanks to Canadian Dave, wherever you are, for telling me to write – about anything and everything – and who said, quite correctly, "You never know what's around the corner." You were more important to me than you probably know.

The story *Inerasable Strokes* was first published in 2003 as *The Wise Man* in *Cadenza* magazine, Issue #8. (*Cadenza* is no longer in print, its strokes erased.)

Printed in Great Britain
by Amazon